The Ghost, Josephine

Brad Rau

—SmallPub—
Portland, ME

For Morgan

The Ghost, Josephine

~

Tonight is warmer than the past week's worth; the sky's clouded over. In an alley beside the Rockland Inn, I empty out the dumpster, tossing heavy, rotten smelling bags into the back of my truck. Ray's waiting in the cab, but with the security light shining past my shoulder, glaring off the rear window, he can't be seen at all.

Winding back to pitch another bag in, the thin plastic splits, spattering trash across the pavement and my boots and the cuff of my pants.

"Goddamn it!" I shout. Kicking the dumpster, I swear again, more colorfully, when a stampede of pain charges through my cold toes, running up my leg. Hopping around, I continue swearing until I've run out of blue words and the pain's dull enough so I can put the foot down again. I can't see Ray, but I can hear him snickering.

A breeze blows down the street, momentarily pushing the stink of garbage away and I hunker down to paw the pile back into the bag, jerking to attention when Sarah Goldstein calls out the kitchen door, "Cookie, Ajna wants you."

She's already gone by the time I turn to her, muttering, "Don't call me..." The door thunks closed.

In the kitchen, Ajna's chopping down chunks of carrot with a cleaver, her nose twitching when I come up beside her. Without turning from her task she tells me, "I need more lobster, Barry." Her accent is riddled with rough, sour r's. In my head her speech looks like the Russian alphabet, backwards r's and n's and the number four as a letter.

"Jesus, Ajna, I just pulled my traps two days ago..."

Ceasing her chopping to lift her head, she still doesn't look at me.

"I mean, sure, I'm happy to try and pull again, but..." I say.

Without even looking at me, the woman—four foot and some inches, probably a third my weight, swaddled in her heavy, drab clothes—manages to dominate me. The way the veins in her neck stand at attention makes me shrink. She pushes the knife down again, dismembering another chunk of carrot, sending it spinning off as the blade cracks down on the board.

"I need the lobsters, Barry. By tomorrow I need twenty lobsters. You need to be here, tomorrow evening with them. No excuses."

The hotel is small and now, with the summer tourist trade having ebbed out entirely, I know there aren't guests enough to eat any twenty lobsters. She's selling them out to someone else—must be. Still, I can't make myself refuse. Maybe it's the accent: a relic of my murky, long-ago childhood, when the inevitability of Soviet attack and that thing on Gorbachev's head were daily news items. Really, it's more than that, though. There's an aura about the woman. I can taste it in the air, it's so thick and grimy.

She lived through that ignored European war of the Nineties and something of that dark time stained her. Stained her right down to her core. So, when she asks for anything, I agree—as quick as I can. And I keep my eyes on her as I retreat outside.

"…And if we can't get them?" Ray asks as we pull out onto Union Street. I don't answer him, but I'm obsessing over what the answer might be.

1

Smacking the side of the boat, the waves sound a slow rhythm; regular and in two beats. Like a heartbeat. Thump-thump. Thump-thump. From a far off buoy, a bell clangs and that sound is bright but lazy and irregular—like the bell can't be bothered. Like there are things the bell would rather be doing.

Pulling hand over hand until the trap breaks the surface of the sea, I drag it in, over the side of the boat. It sloughs water at my feet. Over and above the pissing water, the bell, the heartbeat-waves, is Ray's voice, steady and animated even though I've given him no encouragement, no sign that I'm listening at all.

"…When I hear tires in the gravel out front, she jumps right off me. I've never seen a girl move so fast…"

Our mother said that death couldn't quiet Ray. That not the devil or God Himself could quiet Ray. That his voice was a force, like the wind—given to changing temperaments, but otherwise permanent.

She's dead, our mother. She's quiet and Pa moved south to Florida. He got hot weather, bikinied ladies. I got the old house. I got frozen fingers pulling up lobster traps from an icy October sea. I got Ray. I got Ray's voice talking my ears as numb as my fingers.

Ray is my older brother. He's got fifteen years on me, but you wouldn't know it to see him.

There was no time, for me, when he wasn't around. He's always been there. So constant that I can't be sure of what I'm seeing when I look at him. I know I'm not seeing him, not in the way a stranger might: I can't see him for what he is, because the sight of him is all bound up in the knowledge of him: the man I grew up idolizing, the secrets we share, the lies we honor for one another.

I know him so well that if I wanted to tell you about Ray, I wouldn't know where to begin—what truths to conceal, what tall tales to include. The end result being: I wonder if I could convince you that I know the man at all; that he even exists. I could tell you he's the handsome brother, the talkative brother, the confident one. The brother with all his teeth.

"…So, I'm rushing to gather up this bread-crumb-trail of clothing we left through the house, but Mr. Ernhart's already inside. In the living room…"

This has been going on for hours; Ray talks like this. And then, with the water running around our feet, he quiets. The trap is empty. They've all been empty.

For thirty-five dollars a year a man can keep five traps in the state of Maine. It's what's called a hobby license and if I hadn't gotten myself so dirt poor it might be just that.

We straighten up, Ray and I, standing at once as though only one of us is the man and the other, his reflection. We stand in unison, hands on our hips, frowning down like we're imitating each other, so used to each other's postures and presences that we can't help but mimic. Ray shakes his head and looks at me, clears his throat to continue on. I try and cut him off, but he won't wait, "… He's got his shotgun, right? Raising it up, leveling it out towards me. And I would've ended up full of buckshot, I'm certain of it…"

I raise my hand, open my mouth. Undaunted, Ray keeps going, right over me, "...If at the last moment, he doesn't realize his daughter's bra is hanging off the end of the barrel! Off the end of the shotgun like a goddamned Christmas ornament!" He looks at me, his face punctuating the anecdote, his mouth wide and waiting for me to give a smile. Waves knock the side of the boat. The water in the basin sways.

"I've heard this story," I point out, "So many goddamned times."

Looking at me, his jaw clams up and he gives me the sly smile he tried to earn. "It's a good one, though."

I nod down at the trap again.

He shrugs. "It's empty."

"I know it's goddamned empty, Ray. You think I don't see that?"

"What else to say about it, then? Did I ever tell you about Sharon Wickworth?"

I step back to sit on the overturned milk crate by the motor. The boat's only fourteen feet long. Barely big enough for Ray and me and the empty trap between us. The boat sways. Rockland sits on the horizon, peeking out through a soup of cold fog.

"Fuck Sharon Wickworth," I say. "Ajna Canth is gonna cut off my balls." Gesturing to the floor of the skiff, to the empty trap, to that metaphorical summation and culmination of our empty, fruitless day, I tell him, "Not to mention..." I throw my arms up. "We could've hung drywall today. Hauled trash. That would have been some money. Here... What've we got outta today?"

Ray weighs it. He says, after a moment, "Fresh, salt air. Good for the spirits; that's what Pa always said."

Stomping the water in the basin of the boat so it splashes up on my waders, I yell, "I don't give a good-god-damn about the spirits, Ray. I need to pay some bills."

He shrugs and looks away. Standing again, I take the trap and loll it over the side. It slaps the water and sways, giving in to sinking slowly, like it's settling into bed. As it slips off into the cold, black sea, away from sight, I say, "What about the traps around Owls Head?"

"We don't have traps around Owls Head," Ray tells me. We look at each other a moment before he says, "You trying to get shot?"

"I won't get shot."

Ray nods. "Last summer some dude got shot off Islesboro just for setting his traps in the wrong cove and you think it's a smart idea to go out poaching?"

The motor wakes grudgingly when I yank the cord, coughing and gurgling to life. I aim the boat deeper into the gray sitting away from shore—the gray sky that blends without margin into a gray horizon where one must suspect the sea begins, or ends.

Ray is talking again, but the wind and the motor do a fine job of out-shouting him, so his voice becomes just another layer to the noise, until I'm far away, drifting off in my own thoughts. Ray's yelling brings me back to the world.

There's a big lobster boat not far off, baring down on us. Shaken to, I wrench the motor, cutting out wide, away from the oncoming ship and then turning quickly back into its wake after it's passed.

Bracing against the rollicking-splash, the bow digs into the wave—water coming over us—before the hull rises and we come thudding down on the other side. The boat nods pleasantly—all quiet now with the motor stalled out—and I'm wringing wet, getting to my feet, throttling the air with a fist and letting fly a string of obscenities. I can see her name, *The Bloody Rudder*, as she cruises off into the gray distance.

Lightheaded and shaking, I finally run out of words and breath and sit back down.

"You're gonna blow a gasket, getting worked up like that," Ray tells me when I've stopped panting. In my silence he muses, "Uncle Ernie died from a heart attack. That's in the family."

I pull the starter and the engine gasps to life. "Uncle Ernie smoked three packs a day and ate bacon at every meal."

I can't help, as we come around the jagged, black-rock serration of Owls Head, I can't help but ache over the money wasted on today's venture. Even if we do get every last lobster that I promised Canth, having boated this far will bite into any profit we'll manage. And I've no faith the lobsters will show.

In a little, darkened cove, I hook a buoy with coloring that I don't recognize and snatch the line and pull while Ray looks out. The trap is heavy and when it nears the surface I can see why: it is teeming with lobsters. So much so, that when I latch on and tug, the boat bucks to the side and starts sipping from the surface of the sea. Panicked, I manage to get the trap onboard before we're sunk.

The next five traps we pull aren't so chock-full as that first one, but are full enough to furnish us twice the lobsters Canth demanded. Singing with delight, I do a little jig that gets the boat rocking. I'm smiling all the way back to port.

2

At the public launch we line up behind a big boat just coming free from the water, where the gleaming-red-ghosts of the trailer lights groove. I know the boat. It's out of Minister's Cove, North Haven Island. The fancy, curlycue lettering along the back is easy enough to read even through the gathering dusk. *The Bloody Rudder.* I grind my teeth and wait.

As I stare beyond him, Ray tries catching my eye. He has something he wants to say. The boat pitches and bucks lightly in the waves, while I play the motor back and forth to try and keep still and in the queue—practicing avoiding eye contact with my brother the whole while. Finally, he says, "Let it pass."

I intend to let it pass. But, I don't like being told to. So, I say nothing.

After the *Bloody Rudder* is out, sluicing water as the truck pulls her up the grade, I push our boat forward to land against the dock. Stepping up, out of the boat, I raise my hand dismissively when Ray reminds me, a little louder, "Let it pass."

I intend to let it pass. But coming through the narrow, dirt lot a murmur of conversation followed by a riff of laughter stops me.

I don't quite turn, but my head nods their way to listen. Those boys are quiet now, working in the fragile red glow of trailer lights, readying their boat for the road.

Satisfied that it was only a trick of my imagination, I start forward again, immediately halted by a voice calling, "How was the luck, Cookie?"

On the subdued stage of Autumn dusk that voice sounds shrill; crude. Maybe it's the trumpeting of that voice, maybe it's the little dig of the nickname, whatever it is, I feel my face flush and I turn to the two.

"Fair," I say plainly.

One of them responds but it's quiet—muttered for only the other to hear.

"What's that?" I pipe up.

They rearrange themselves, standing tall and glaring me down. "I said," a voice chimes through the darkness. I need to count on the movement of his body to determine which one is speaking. "It's a funny word for you to use—fair."

"What the fuck's that supposed to mean?"

The quieter boy speaks up now. "Nothing, Barry. Take it easy. Keep moving."

"Easy?" I say. "You're the ones yelling at me. If you got something to say, say it."

"I'll say it!" The loud boy says, dropping down off the trailer and stepping closer. Gravel cackles under his feet. "It's bullshit, you coming in with a goddamned haul. You don't hold a single trap at Owls Head. Everybody knows that."

When I say again, "What the fuck's that supposed to mean?" I'm moving too. Only when we're closer—coming closer with every breath and step and I have him half-silhouetted with the tail lights from his trailer—can I see that he has some long armament hanging from his hand. I come to a stop.

He stops, too—a few paces out. "You're a fucking thief, Cookie. Everyone knows it." He aims the tire iron at me.

"Yeah?" My face is hot enough now so that my eyes are getting watery. "Yeah?" I say though my teeth.

"Yeah," he says, real quiet.

Night has congealed around us. There is only a long blue strip of day left across the horizon and it is in hurried retreat, slipping away across the earth, maybe in New Hampshire now. Maybe Vermont. The man standing in front of me is all nighttime—a man-shaped-cutout of nighttime—black and flat, eclipsing the red of the taillights. A little red hangs onto the feathery edge of his sweater. The fleece shimmers in the wind.

"Come on," the brother insists impatiently. "We don't have time for this."

"One second, Todd," the boy before me says over his shoulder. Turning back to me he huffs, "You're lucky you weren't into our traps. You're lucky I have respect for the Andrews family." He says, almost whispering now, "You're just a piece-of-shit-thief, anyways. Not even worth my time."

I do not plan any of this; simply moving, like a cat on the Savannah. He's turned and before he's landed a full step toward his truck I'm leaning down and taking a fist sized rock from the ground by my feet and before I've thought or breathed or pumped a solitary heartbeat, my hand is coming back and, without cognition or reasoning, the hand has already started forward again and the pebble, the stone—it's a rock, really: big enough to crush a skull, big enough to buckle a truck door—is free from my hand. Given fully to the air.

Maybe I'm lucky I was never an athlete. Well over six foot tall, bulky and strong, these aspects are largely experienced by the world as varying degrees of clumsiness. Todd's brother is, without a doubt, lucky I was never an athlete: though I have aimed for his head, the rock has a path of its own, that curves with a significant downward arc, hitting him dead center of his left ass cheek. Twisting and pitching, he lets fly a sour sort of grunt before I hear the tire-iron clang, bell-like, on the frozen ground.

The boy falls to a knee and I'm still moving forward, like the cheetah, not toward him now, but past him, toward Todd who's dropped down, off the trailer—launching himself forward like another predatory cat. I can hear him let out his war-cry as he comes on: we are two cats playing chicken. My feet leave the ground, diving forward, aiming low at the last moment, taking him out across the midsection. Todd's war-cry deflates. We hit the ground together, rolling, and somehow I manage to get on top. Aiming for his chin, I jab forward into the darkness beneath me, missing— but only the darkness knows by how much.

Behind me I hear the bright scraping of metal against cold stone. Knowing the younger brother is back up and on his way, I have to accept that missed-punch as the only shot I'll get. I roll off Todd and away. There is a quiet, invisible form breaking through the darkness, and I'm only half risen when I reach up, blindly catching the tire iron as it comes down. I wrench it free from him, staggering up to my feet. Todd's brother falls away into the blackness behind me.

The ground is quiet: no crunching footsteps any more, just the heavy hush of panted breath. They both, at once, seem to realize what's happened: that now, with the tire iron, I firmly have the upper hand.

Without discussion, they back-step toward their truck, light glaring across the lot when the doors pop open and they jump in. And I realize, just in this moment, that I am screaming like a maniac.

The hull of the boat gets smacked with debris as the tires tear into the dirt and the whole rig jerks forward, pulling away. I'm still screaming as I cast the tire iron aside. Then I'm left alone, panting in the resumed, crystalline silence; ragged breathed, worn.

"Jesus Christ, Ray," I say when he jogs up beside me. "Good fucking timing."

"I came when I heard you yell."

By the time I pull the truck down the ramp, load up and lash down our boat and pull out onto Route One, Ray is yammering on about some other girl, April something-or-other. Interrupting him I say, "What the fuck took you so long?" It isn't a question, it isn't a statement—I can't help the hurt in my voice.

Ray says, "I had to secure the boat."

"How long's that goddamned take?"

"I think everything happened a bit quicker than you think it did, little brother."

"Well," I say. "It would have been nice if you'd made an effort."

He sighs. "I told you to let it pass. Fuck, maybe when I heard you yell I didn't rush right over. Maybe I rolled my eyes a little beforehand. You don't listen to advice. What am I supposed to do?"

In Meredith's driveway, Ray sits silent a moment. "Tomorrow?" he asks.

"If there's work."

"Don't be all pissy."

"I ain't all pissy," I say, a pissy strain in my voice.

"Okay. I'll see you tomorrow," he says, reaching for the handle.

I tell him, "It costs me to come out here. It's gas, you know."

He nods. "Something will come up. We'll figure it out. We always do."

I say, "I can't just hang out. I need to make money, Ray."

He says nothing.

We both turn when Meredith's shape appears in the front door of the house.

"I should go," I say, reaching to put the truck in gear.

"Say hello. Don't be a fucking weirdo," he nods at me, pats the door—thump, thump—slipping out and falling off into the darkness. Then Meredith's rapping at my window and I know it's too late. I let my hand drop to the crank and wind the window halfway down.

"Hey Barry, whatcha doin'?"

"Going over to the Inn."

It takes her a moment; looking back at the boat, she says. "Where you coming from?"

"The bay."

"This way?"

"I should go," I tell her.

She laughs. "You only just rolled in," she says and laughs. "Come in for a beer, hang out a bit. I haven't seen you in awhile."

"I gotta go," I say and put the truck in reverse. It bucks eagerly, ready to go.

Meredith looks at me. Blinking weirdly, she steps back from the door of the truck, consumed almost instantly by darkness. "Good seeing you, Barry," the nighttime tells me in her voice. Moments later the door to the house opens again, throwing light across the dooryard and the tangle of her and Ray's shadows slip inside. And I am alone.

3

Finished counting the lobsters out, having weighed them on her skewed scale and entered some marks in a ledger that are a mystery to me, Ajna Canth mutters in her mangled English, "It's more than I asked for."

"We settled on two dollars a pound," I say and I have to clench my jaw to keep the apologetic 'I'd thought,' from worming it's way out. I have to be strong. She'll cheat me if I'm not. Honestly, she's going to cheat me regardless; all I can do is damage control, try to keep my losses minimal.

Turning to regard the coolers on the countertop by her side she touches her fingertips to her lips, shakes her head thoughtfully. When her gaze isn't on me I straighten. But when she looks back again I flinch, my posture failing, like a man about to puke. A smile creases her face—only there a moment and then gone like a ghost.

The kitchen is empty—quiet but for the lobsters tapping mutedly on the other side of that narrow styrofoam wall. From a guest room above there's a dull drone of conversation. Behind me, the cricket-song of refrigerators.

Shrugging, Ajna says, "What would I do with so many?"

"Whatever you always do. There's never been an issue with..."

"But, so much, Barry," she says, eyeing again the coolers. "Too much. I can take them, but only as a favor to you. I won't use them all and I can't pay more."

Determined not to be swindled by the ninety-five pound Croat again, I counter, "No," as firmly as my throat will allow. The word comes out weaselly.

Her eyes are dead-gray, but again her smile surfaces. It rings as a taunt, when she says, "No?"

"I'll get a fair price, thank you."

It's not a question; it's a dare, a challenge when she says, "You take them somewhere else?"

"Fine," I say, but she blocks my path when I step forward. Now, here, the smile is evident—put on for me to see when whispering my name, "Barry."

I've back-peddled. She's willed me to the place where I started. I manage not to look away while she studies me, but it takes effort. When my head starts getting light, I realize I've been holding my breath.

"I wouldn't cheat you, Barry. You come here to do business. And we are friends."

We are not friends. I nod.

"Grappa."

I shake my head.

She nods. "Grappa." Stepping away, she returns with two small glasses and a narrow bottle. Normally, this is reserved for the end of our dealings and the fact that it's coming early makes me nervous. Like maybe she's planning on killing me.

I don't know what Grappa is. I suspect it is rubbing alcohol. Or poison. Maybe both, mixed together for dilution. It tastes like industrial solvent. We drink, her lips parting as though for a kiss, her eyes delicately closing to savor. I swallow hard, staring at her.

Her throat is pale and the skin is thin enough so that I can see the webbing of black veins beneath. She would kill me with a knife, I think, kill me if she thought she could get away with it. Over those lobsters in the cheap styrofoam box, she would gut me. Probably over less. But she knows, we both know: she's too small to drag my body anywhere. That simple reality keeps me alive right now, I'm sure.

Showing her smile again—little teeth, almost brown—she gestures with the bottle. I shake my head, no, and she says, "Business. The problem: I didn't ask for so many. You see the problem. I do not have money for this many. This is the problem."

"Take the half we arranged for and I'll take the rest back."

"Back to the ocean? What?" There's a momentary panic in her fluttering eyes when I step forward again. "Fine. It would be fine for Ajna. But, what about Barry? What will Barry do with the other half? Out all night selling lobsters," she says, eyeing me.

"Maybe I'll take them home. Eat them myself," I say. "It doesn't matter. It isn't your concern."

"But, Barry doesn't like lobster."

Weird, giant, prehistoric bugs. Eyes wandering out of their strange, hooded skulls. Perhaps it's a form of sacrilege, being a native Mainer and detesting sea-spiders. I wish I'd never told her how they make my skin crawl. It's another weapon in the arsenal she has against me. I say, again, "It isn't your concern what I do with them."

Clucking her tongue, she shakes her head and repeats, "Out all night selling lobsters." Giving pause to think it over and then, leaning in closer, she whispers, "Stolen lobsters," shaking her head, as though ashamed for me.

I feel my face flush. "I didn't steal."

She shrugs, doesn't care. "So many rumors. So many things said about Barry. Only Ajna sticks up for Barry. No one else."

Though I've said nothing, my face burns and I know that that has told all—I've sold myself out. "Two dollars a pound for the half we agreed on. What are you offering for the other half?"

"I don't have the kind of money you're asking for." She turns up her hands.

"I haven't asked. I want to know what you're offering."

She makes a big act of mulling it, but I know she's only pausing, not giving it any thought at all, before she says, "Fifty."

"Cents? A pound? That's cheaper than liver. Cheaper than bones. I'll take them home."

Again she sidesteps, blocking my path. There is no smile this time. We've come down to money now. The risk to my life is tangible—material.

"Seventy five," she says. The words are husky, whispered low, mired in an accent that has gotten thicker; twisting up the words.

"A dollar."

Her bony, little hands wring quickly and curl closed. "Eighty."

"I won't take less than a dollar. I won't be made to count coins." I'm sweating. My hands are damp. The collar of my shirt is damp. This could be the closest that I have stood to death and I have stood very close to death, you could ask my brother.

I let a moment pass. She's fuming-pissed. She's a goddamned oven, simmering with quiet, steel-still rage. Softly, plainly, I say, "Or, I can take them elsewhere."

I get my sixty-four dollars handed out in pained accounting—each bill smacked on the countertop as though an act of vengeance—the dollars rolling out to me from a bundle that looks far from exhausted when she's finished. I know it's intentional, her allowing me to see it. She wants me to know that I didn't win. That I didn't get the best of her. I do.

I'm not gloating with success, I'm barely holding it together when I cross through the kitchen toward the door, knowing that for days I will obsess over how badly I was cheated. With Ajna, even success is defeat. Right now, though, I just want to get free, even if it means leaving my back exposed to the Croat.

Ajna's voice stops me at the door. Radiating through the handle, the frigid Autumn night tempts me out; promising that I'll be snugger with her than inside the warm hotel with Ajna.

"Barry," she says. Her renewed, crooning tone sends a cold wave of dread through me. Turned back to face her, I catch sight of the twenty-dollar-bill in her hand. "There's other work for you."

I've turned, but even the monumental gravity of that twenty-spot isn't enough to get me moving again. She must, I realize, have some horrendously lowly act for me to perform to warrant such a fee. I say, "What work?"

"You must promise me."

"Promise you what?"

Setting the bill on the counter, sliding it in my direction with her tented, arachnid fingers, she finally steps aside but I dare not move. This is almost certainly a trap; my potential movement an invitation for her knife. I can imagine it perfectly enough, buried to the hilt in my gut-fat. "Barry, I think you do not trust me."

"What work?"

"Take the money and promise," she says and allows for an inviting moment and when I do not take it, when I still do not move, she says, "This promise. I must have your loyalty. You work for me, you only take money from me. We are partners. We split everything fifty-fifty. I will be your..."

"Pimp," I say.

She smiles—enjoying the word, the ring of it, thinking it might suit her, but unwilling to let me be the one to bestow it. "Agent," she corrects.

"Nicer word."

"Do you want the work?" she asks and she isn't asking if I want the work, but if I need the money and, sourly, the answer is yes. I trundle forward, back across the tiled floor to the counter, slipping the bill into my pocket without ever-once looking at it; as though I'm thieving on the sly. The scar of her smile deepens.

4

Passing through the swinging doors I realize that I've never seen anything of the hotel, beyond the narrow, fastidiously kept kitchen.

In the hallway, in the lobby beyond, the rugs covering the floors seem too big for the spaces they inhabit—too big, too ornate; old and worn. Everything has that look. Brass and dark-wood and heavy shadows settled in the corners—it is a place from another age where rooms were small and cluttered-full with claustrophobic patterns. The glittering eyes of a taxidermied bunny-head flash at me as I pass.

When Ajna pivots the banister and starts upstairs, I feel my legs weaken and I come to a stop. A fog of melancholy, almost completely opaque, guards the threshold, blocking my path.

I made the wrong decision taking her money. I know that now.

A few steps above me, our faces on level, Ajna turns back to command, "Come."

I finger the bill in my pocket. I could slide it free, let it loose. Let it drift to the ground. Turn. Leave. Never come back. Rather than rising, her voice drops. "You cannot stand there." I step forward into the gloom, onto the first stair. And it's suddenly too late to turn back. The wallpaper on the second floor greets me like sea-serpent-tentacles, pulling me in, dragging me down to the farthest door in the hallway where Ajna steps aside. When I hesitate again she says, "Through," brusquely.

"Who's in there?"

"Through," she says again and I step through. Beyond the door is a narrow flight of stairs, leading up. I climb up into an attic room.

Like what I've already seen of the hotel, the room I emerge into is narrow, dark and cluttered; an old smell steeped into everything. At first, not recognizing the man in the chair before me seems a relief, but as he starts his silent appraisal the feeling erodes.

We watch each other.

"How much did she give you?" He narrows his eyes as though speaking is a discomfort. I say nothing. "I gave her a fifty to pass along. Did she give you that?"

A bed on one side of the room looks untouched—the quilt across it as uniform as cured concrete. There has been an effort made to furnish the room to the point of bursting. The nameless man before me sits in one of two big wicker chairs that dominates what floor space the bed doesn't occupy. A coffee table rigged from a lobster trap and a slab of glass is wedged between the chairs. The sight of the trap makes my lip curl—acid rising in my gut.

"Have a seat." Leaning to the side, he dislodges a wallet from his pocket. Searching a moment, he lays a bill out atop the table. I come and sit. The bill is a fifty. The acid in my belly abates. Something inside me wriggles nervously, like it wants to be happy but can't commit.

"Take it."

Pocketing the bill, I announce, "I don't do sex stuff. Not with dudes."

He cringes, looking away. "I wouldn't be interested if you did; I wouldn't want to hear about it if you did." His face is hard; the face of a man who routinely violates one principle in order to maintain another; the face of a man who does so without conflict or question; the face of a man who weighs out decisions in an instant.

I tell him, "I don't sell drugs, either."

"I'm not into drugs."

I shrug. "If you are, I can get you some. But, it'll cost."

We're both silent for the moment it takes him to tamp down a pack of Dunhill's. Lighting up, the little room fills instantly with smoke. He looks at the cigarette in his fingers. "I told you I'm not into drugs. You ever a smoker?"

"In high school, socially. Not since."

"I quit twenty-five years. Had one and it was like I'd never quit at all. Went right back. Pack a day."

"That's expensive."

"I don't have to worry about money. Not that kind of money, anyway." He exhales. A noxious pillow of smoke plows over me. I close my eyes. When I open them again he says, "Nobody ever wishes to be poor. That said, being rich isn't great either. You have more money—less time, it seems. You spend your time worrying about your money."

"Hard life."

"I'm just explaining to you how it is," he says.

"I'll tell you how it is." Something in the way he's sitting and looking me over is rubbing a raw nerve, deep down. "I'm so poor that when I told you I don't do sex shit, I had to wonder if I was lying." I look at him—serving back his practiced stare. After he's said nothing, I say, "I do some construction around here. In the area. Big houses. Houses built for rich people. People like you. You know what I think about in big, empty houses? I think: these rooms aren't for people—they're for egos. But, you know what? I don't care how big your bathroom is, fuck-head, you're still dropping trow, and laying brown-pipe like every other filthy mammal on the goddamned planet. No matter how big the room gets, you're still sitting over your own fresh-baked, steaming butt-bread. No amount of money can reverse the reality that you're not actually better than anyone else. You just have more stuff."

There's a look on his face: twisted up. Hard to tell if he's come to respect me, or is already worn out on me—already through talking with me. He holds the expression. "Butt-bread? Never heard that one. You came up here for fifty bucks. You sat for another fifty. What's it gonna cost to get a civil conversation from you?"

"I only got twenty to come up here." Smiling, I show him my missing tooth. I start to stand, stopping when I see him spread four fifties out on the tabletop.

He keeps his hand on the bills, his eyes locked on mine. "That get your attention?"

When he pulls his hand away I ease back into the chair. I don't reach for the money, but I can't take my eyes from it either.

"I worry," I tell him. "What you'd be paying me for, if you're willing to pay so much."

"Civil conversation," he says. "For now, civil conversation."

"In the future?"

"No one knows the future." He looks at me. He smiles. "Or is that not quite true? I've heard tell you have a window to it."

I just stare back at him. His smile dies. He settles back in his chair.

"You were in jail some years ago. How long did you serve?"

When he doesn't acknowledge that my hand's landed on the cash, I scoop it up and jam it into my pocket. My heart is beating so hard, I worry he can hear it. "Five months."

"Breaking and entering."

"If you knew, why'd you ask? It was a misunderstanding. I was drunk; stumbled into the wrong place."

"That a lie?"

"Maybe. But, I already have your money."

He nods, considering it. "This is a test. To see if you can be trusted for the work I need done. Maybe you should think about that before opening your mouth up again. How many homes have you robbed?"

Not that many. I could count them out, if I tried; probably count them on one hand, plus a few fingers from the other. But, I don't say that to him. Instead, I say, "I can't answer that question."

"You're not interested in making more money?" he asks, nodding to the empty place on the table where his cash had been.

"I'm interested in money," I tell him. "I'm not interested in returning to jail."

"I'm not a cop."

"I appreciate you saying that, but it's more an issue of confidence than reassurances."

He nods. "I understand." Clearing his throat, shifting in his chair, he stubs out his cigarette on the bottom of his shoe. Ash and ember drift to the floor as he sets the smoldering butt on the table between us, immediately sparking up another as the glass-top starts to blacken. I wait, watching as he examines the glowing ember of his fresh cigarette. He says, "Let me tell you about myself, then."

"If you think that's worth my time and your money. You can talk all you want but I'll tell you right now, there's no one in my life I trust well enough to share with, what you've asked me to share." I think of Ray because he's the one who knows all my secrets, knows me through and through, but I won't speak his name. Not here. I say, "No one."

The man across from me weighs this. Having come to some sort of conclusion, he says, "I'll tell you about myself. And when I tell you about myself you'll understand why I've sought you out and you'll know you can trust me. You'll know what I want, and once you know that you'll know the very marrow of my being—everything I've ever been and all that I can ever be."

"Is that gonna take long?"

His face puckering into a near-snarl, he says, "If I am honest with you, I expect you to be honest with me."

"If you're honest."

"You'll know. You'll know I'm honest," he says. The ash on his cigarette is growing. He holds it out, away from the chair and flicks it toward the floor, taking a puff to tell me, "I am this cigarette."

"I'm not sure that qualifies as honest." I shrug. "I'm pretty certain it isn't true, at any rate."

His eyes shine, a dark glimmer. "I didn't smoke for thirty years."

"I thought it was twenty-five."

"It was a long time," he says impatiently. "I quit when my wife quit. Our daughter's name was Josephine..."

I have already started standing and he trails off, watching me rise. He was right. I do know him. I know him already and I know he's telling me the truth and I know exactly what he wants from me. And I know he's honest. And I know it's all he has, just as he's claimed. Shaking my head, I say, "You're better off keeping your money."

"But, my daughter..."

"Your daughter's gone. No one can reverse that. Not me—not anyone."

"But, you..." he stammers. His voice is shimmering, plaintive, fragile. It breaks my heart.

"No," I tell him. Digging his money out of my pocket, I toss it back onto the coffee table. A few bills slip off onto the floor. "I never did what they claim I did. It was a hoax. The whole thing. Keep your money."

"You're lying," he says, the delicate nature of his grief eroding; I can see the anger now, the frustration bubbling up in his face. It just makes me feel worse for him.

"It doesn't matter. I won't help you."

"I thought you said 'can't.'"

"It's the same answer, no matter how I word it," I say. I've been through this a few times now. And it's always like this, more or less. Some sad, sick person crawls out of his grief long enough to convince himself that I can help. That somehow, this person he's meeting—me—whom he's never met, that was famous for five minutes two decades ago can somehow fix what's broken in his life. I cannot. And—maybe the saddest part is—even if I could, I wouldn't.

"I paid you. Stay and listen."

I shake my head, no. I tell him, "No."

"I need to tell you about Josephine."

"I don't want to hear about your daughter."

"It's five thousand dollars."

"That isn't enough."

"Seven... Ten, then. Ten thousand."

I shake my head. "It doesn't matter how much it is. It won't be enough."

"Everyone has a price."

"It's yours, you see; no one can heal your grief but you. You own it and it isn't something you can sell away."

"This isn't about grief. She's killing me; trying to ruin me," he says.

I've already turned away. The last word I hear from him is, "Please."

5

I shower under a spray so cold it feels like pebbles lashing me. Dressed, I jog in place, punching the air to get my blood going. Without the hum of the refrigerator, without the knock and groan of the radiator, the house is ghostly quiet.

Outside, Ray's waiting for me. "Didn't want you to waste gas coming to get me," he says as I breeze past, climbing into the pickup. The windshield's gray-laced with frost. After getting the truck started I turn the defrost on high. I blow into my hands and wring them, trying to push the nagging cold from my digits. Ray says, "You're welcome. I walked. Don't worry, it's not that cold out."

I roll my eyes, making fists with my hands. "You want cold, go inside for five minutes."

"You're a peach this morning."

"House is a goddamned ice box. Pa was right moving."

"Pa? Pa's turned sissy in his old age. This here, Barry, is fucking weather. This is goddamned weather. This is what the pilgrims traveled to get a taste of."

"That may have been more an issue of religious freedom, I've been told."

He shrugs. "Call it what you will. Historians will tell you they came for God. History will tell you they got New England weather. Who are either of us to speak for them about what it was they were after?" He's full of it this morning. Talking like a flood-river emptying into the sea. I should be happy he isn't on a tangent about some long-lost ex of his. I should be happy for the reprieve. After a moment, he says, "Or, you could move to Florida. Sell the house and move. That's probably what you should do. Have you talked to Pa recently?"

The frost on the windshield is fragile, eaten away quickly by the blowing fan and, with a little half-dome nine inches tall to see through, I put the truck in gear and start out onto the road. After less than a moment of silence has elapsed, he starts, "Suzy Trask..."

"Jesus, Ray. Can we not do this today?"

"What do you mean: this?"

"This thing where I spend the whole day listening to you jabber about girls... Girls from your past, girls you had, girls you wished you had. Girls you dreamt about, girls you looked at, girls you touched. Girls. That thing. This. You know, Ray? There's more to talk about than just women."

"I tried talking about pilgrims. You didn't seem keen on that, either."

"I don't wanna talk about pilgrims, Ray."

"Okay. What'd you want to talk about?"

"What are we doing for work?" I say. "Where the fuck are we gonna find work?"

"Is your thinking that this will be a more pleasant conversation? 'Cause it sounds depressing and, at any rate, it's probably a talk we should've started before leaving the driveway." He looks down the road as I turn the truck off onto a narrow, rutted pass that cuts out into the woods. Imprinted with the chunky tread marks of construction vehicles, the gravel and dirt is bucked up into big ruts. "The McKier job. So you do know where we're going for work; that was your attempt at conversation."

"We're going to the McKier job to see if we can land work for the day. I'm talking about long term goals."

"Long term goals. Good. Whatcha got?"

Stopping the truck just beyond the curtain of the woods, I can see the house (just a damp framework of two-bys) is empty; the muddy lot around it, empty. A flag of plastic sheeting whips in and out of a hole where a window should go.

Ray says, "No one's here."

"I see that," I tell him. Pulling closer to the house and killing the engine, the resulting silence is staggering. It's cold out, but the gas gauge is too low to risk running the truck for heat.

"Suzy Trask..."

"No," I say. "No. No. No. I told you, we're not doing this."

We're quiet awhile, looking at the house. Looking in through the yawning doorframe, the floor inside is littered with wet leaves. It doesn't look like anyone's been here for days, weeks. Maybe longer. "They're not coming, are they?"

"No," Ray says. "They're not coming. At least we made money yesterday."

"And I still don't have enough to get the electricity turned back on, or the oil tank filled. This isn't a solution, us floundering like this. Chasing all these odd jobs. Living just gets leaner and leaner. And what are we headed towards?"

We sit because neither one of us can come up with anywhere to go where there might-be-money-to-be-made and being outside, in the sun is reasonably less depressing than going home to a house without lights or heat. At one point Ray offers, "We could go to Meredith's. It's warm there, even if there's no cable."

I shake my head.

"She's at work."

I shake my head again.

"We could drive around a bit."

I tap the dashboard over the fuel gauge.

When Ray starts up again, "Suzy Trask..." I open the door and drop out into the day.

Walking through the woods around the house I kick at wet piles of leaves and, in my most productive moment, push the tall stump of a big, rotted birch over. The soft fiber makes a papery sound as it gives way. It takes me right back to being a kid— spreading a big smile over my face. Makes me remember romping through the woods behind our house. Coming home to Meredith getting dinner ready. She wasn't much older than I was. Old enough so that Pa trusted her cooking; old enough so she didn't look like a child to Ray, I suppose. Then I remember, I'm no kid at all. Not anymore. I'm a thirty-seven year old man with no electricity, no job, no prospects.

Past noon, I return to the pickup. We play cribbage with a deck of cards from the glovebox, summing points on the back of a receipt as the day thins out into shadows. Then, finally, it gets too cold to sit any longer, too dim to see the suits. The day has all but evaporated. I start up the truck. The lights flash starkly against the geometric perfection of the unfinished house, against the chaotic scrimshaw of trees behind it. Pulling back out onto the street I try not to think about what a waste today has been.

And then, laboring not to think about it—I'm thinking about it again. Thinking about the electricity; about how far I am, even with getting paid last night, from having the utilities settled out. The nights are already aching cold a week into October. I'm thinking how screwed I'll be if I let it get to November without power, the December afterward. The long, agonizing tundra of January, February, March and half of April still ahead. Then all this turns from a sad experiment in minimalism to burst pipes and frost bite. To a house surrendered to deterioration. Then, I'm done.

Without having settled on it, or so much as discussed it, I find myself aiming the truck toward the wealthy enclave of Camden. The wind has started up; the trees sway blackly against a deep blue sky.

6

"I thought you were worried about gas," Ray says, and when I say nothing he says, "Have we given up on conversation, then?" I keep quiet, eyes on the grimy windscreen. "It just seems like you've made up your mind about something and as your partner..."

"Partner?"

"Accomplice. Brother. Whatever. It just seems to me that if you're making up your mind about something you should at least fill me in. That if you're making up your mind over something, you should put it to a vote."

"I've never known you to say no," I tell him.

"Maybe I'd like the opportunity to," Ray says.

Taking the turns slowly, carefully: maybe that's how he knows I've made up my mind. Maybe it's just that he's my brother. I turn off onto a road that hugs the coast. The driveways out here are far apart, some of them fancy-brick-laid, some of them gated.

The truck lights fall over a tall, ornate privacy fence, and I think about how a single panel probably costs enough to straighten out my utility woes. He says, "Maybe I'd just like the option of talking you out of something you'll regret."

I say, "I don't know what choice I have, Ray. I can't let it get into November without electricity; with no hot water. With no fucking heat. What choice is there?" I ask, but I know what choice there is—I'm thinking about the man at the Rockland Inn, wondering if he could actually get me the kind of money he said he could. Though, as soon as the thought arises, it gives bloom to a sick feeling in the pit of my stomach. Looking at Ray the sickness is ripe enough to worry about it blossoming up my throat.

"Meredith would put you up in a heartbeat."

"That's no kinda solution," I tell him, before even considering whether it might be. "What about Pa's house? Our ancestral home."

He laughs. "You make it sound like Buckingham Palace. It's a shotgun shack."

"It's our home," I say.

"Pa's gone. It's your house. Yours to sell. Sell it. It isn't worth keeping. Especially, if it means..." he nods out to the rooftop beyond the fence.

I don't say anything. Fact is, without the house, what do I have in this earthly world?. This junk truck, armfuls of debt, a fourteen foot fiberglass boat, clothes going to rags. It isn't anything. Nothing worth a damn.

Ray says, "I don't think the risk is worth the reward."

"Yesterday you were all for nicking traps and now you're making a stink over... What?"

He sighs. "I don't remember being 'all for that,' either."

He knows about the man at the Rockland Inn, I'm sure. He's gonna try to talk me into going back there, taking that offer. I stare at him. He says nothing for a moment, finally saying, "What if you're caught?"

"Jail," I say. "Won't have to worry about the heat then."

He nods. "Right. Just worry about getting punked in the ass."

"Nobody's punkin' anybody," I say. With the truck off the road, half-tucked into the woods, I cut the lights and kill the engine. In the distance the slate rooftop glimmers dimly. The windows peering over the fence are dark.

Ray says, "I'm not sure this one's empty, Barry."

"It's empty. The lights are off. It's seven-thirty. It's empty."

"It looks haunted."

"They all look haunted when they're huge and empty," I say. I say, "Come on," and I climb out from the cab.

The night is crazy; the wind blowing the trees around and the booming of the ocean like a warning of something terrible and inevitable stomping its way toward me. We dart across the street together and I take a big, energetic leap at the fence but my leaping isn't what it once was so, with upheld arms, I hit the fence hard and slide off.

Ray is still laughing when I try the move again, this time managing to latch hold of the top of the fence and pull myself up. There's much grunting involved. Squirming and wriggling I scrape the inside of my thigh and crush my junk and fall to the ground, a graceless tangle of ache. Ray is still laughing.

"Fuck you."

"You are so out of shape."

"I'm bigger than you, so fuck off."

He's still laughing.

The house is dark; so dark that the panes of the windows manage to find smudges of light from the nighttime and reflect them back, though wherever this source of light is, is a mystery to me. Ray says, "I'm still not sure it's empty."

"You're nuts," I tell him. "'Course it's empty. Look at it."

Ray's not the only one who feels it. Starting around the house, I'm feeling it too: something is wrong. Like I'm being watched. But the house is dark and I've made such an argument of my certainty, now I feel bound to it. Negotiating my approach, I duck from hedge to hedge like I'm coming up on something dangerous and asleep.

The house is huge, a confusion of windows looking out. But, for some reason it takes a lot of searching before I find the one I like. It's low and wide and it's the only one I come upon that offers more to see inside than impenetrable pitch. A grand piano cowers in a corner, behind it a wall of books. I find a stone by my feet and with a quick, crystalline splash the window dissolves. I clear out the sill with the rock. Hesitant a moment, I stand, looking in and listening. The ocean crashes. The wind swooshes in the trees.

The drapes framing the window writhe as I lay my hands on the sill and hoist myself in. Before moving on I turn, wiping the window down with my sleeve and thinking I should steal some gloves, maybe a hat, maybe a pillowcase for a bag. My lack of preparedness is embarrassing.

Quiet and still, the house invites me further in. Maybe it's the silence that causes me to sneak, but—some paces in—I'm frozen when a peal of laughter rings down the hall. A sheen of sweat materializes instantly over me. Unable to move or even think for a moment, except to hear the voice screaming in my head, "God damn it, Ray was right," I stare into the gloomy hallway ahead. Suddenly, the prospect of jail seems tangible, nearly inevitable.

It's Ray who pipes up first. "Fuck."

The word is like a cattle prod, jarring me back into motion and I start back-stepping, whispering urgently, "Let's go. Let's get out of here."

"Fuck," Ray says again and when I turn I find that he hasn't retreated a pace. Standing rigid, his face is twisted up in an expression of shock and, following his gaze to the doorway, I see now, there in that miry darkness, what was hidden before. In the blackness before us, two white eyes blink calmly, watching Ray. A blanket draped over his arm, three digits of a hand stuffed into his mouth, the little boy steps into the relative light of the big room around us.

Removing the hand from his mouth, turning to face me, the child asks, "Are you here to turn the lights back on?"

Relief briefly floods in. "Yup. Yup. Here to turn the power on. I just need..." Resuming my retreat, I say, "To look at this switch over here."

The child watches. His wide-opened-eyes are impossibly bright through the darkness. In my careful back-peddling, I'm aware of (not hearing for the first time, but for the first time really aware of) a voice calling, "Gregory? Gregory?"

And, as if that name is an incantation, bringing form into the world—suddenly, in the same dark doorway a woman appears. In the cast of the milky light coming through the window, she stops—just as the boy had. Her eyes are wider and even brighter than his. Raising my hand, as though in apology, I find myself frozen-still once more. She's the first to move, grabbing the boy, pulling him back into the darkness. At once, as though agreed upon, Ray and I spring into action, jumping back, through the window.

Launching myself outside, a little tooth of glass from the windowsill bites my hand. Blood starts down my fingers the moment my feet hit the ground. Breaking into an all-out sprint, I cut across the yard, running myself so hard that within the first few paces I'm already winded.

Lightheaded and full of dread, I realize I've only brokered a quarter of the lawn when I begin to have doubts about my escape-readiness. I should have paced myself.

And that's when I hear the dogs. How many of them, what breed, I can't discern from their yapping and growling, but in my mind they are at least five, maybe seven strong, a threatening mix of mastiffs and dobermans and pit bulls, all frothy mouthed with thirsty-rage.

Up ahead the fence is bobbing closer, just beyond an apple tree. Having covered half the lawn, the dogs' barking is already unbearably loud. They're right on top of me—at my ankles. I jump, grabbing a tree limb and yanking myself up, just as a dog's muzzle brushes my foot.

Jail, I think. Boredom and danger. Desperation. But, at least I'm not dog food. My heart almost chokes, suddenly overfull with shame as I climb, groaning, "Uuuuuggghhh."

By the time I realize that I've been cornered by a pekingese and two aged border collies, it's too late. A man's already crossing the lawn toward me. I'm already in the beam of his flashlight. The barrel of his rifle peeks out, bobbing along with him as he says, over the frail barking of the ancient dogs, "Stay where you are. The police are on their way." Shadows from the tree limbs tattoo my sleeves and belly and face and rotate dizzyingly as he advances, like the branches are seizing me—holding me for him.

2

"You're going to pay me back," Meredith says. It's the first thing she's said as we drive through the long, low fields, away from the Knox County Jail. It's a bright day. Bright and cold and my insides are filled with similar, bitter contradictions after a long week inside. And, while I'm happy to be driving into the constrictions of court-approved freedom, the future I'm headed for can't be seen as anything more than vague and dismal. Lawyers fees, fines, an almost-certain, extended jail stay awaiting me in the not so distant future; my prospects have, somehow, gotten worse. "What the heck were you thinking, Barry?"

"You'll get your money back when I go to the hearing."

"You better show. If you don't show I swear I'll hunt you down," she says and then repeats the phrase, "Hunt you down," as though for emphasis, but it's barely loud enough to hear.

When I reach for the radio dial she smacks my hand away, scolding, "Nope." But, then it becomes less apparent who she's scolding when she says, "No, no, no. You're not my child." Her saying that only manages to deepen the raw teenage-embarrassment that I'm feeling; shamed and without good answers to give and knowing that I've fucked up royally and wishing there was some fantastic way I could go back in time; wishing I could make different choices. I say, "I owe you."

The tires warble over the pavement while I watch out the window. Beside the road the grass is still green, but there's not a leaf left on the trees beyond.

"Yeah. You do." She sighs, shakes her head. After a moment she says again, "What were you thinking?"

It sort-of shocks me when I lament aloud, "I'm gonna lose the house."

"Yeah. I'd say that's the least of your worries. You oughta sell it, Barry. Get the money, get a lawyer. Or, take the plea. That's what you should do. Take the plea. Whatever they offer." Pinching her eyes shut a moment, she rubs her forehead. Looking back to the road she sighs. "I don't even know what that means: take the plea. I think I heard it on a cop show."

I tune her out. I don't want to dwell on any of this. I wanna get the cash from the house, go to a cheap hotel, get drunk and take a hot shower. Wash away my sins, inside and out. Put on clean clothes. My shirtsleeve is stained—old blood now, gone brown—from having cut myself on the Farmer's window. That was their name. The damned, shitty irony. Their name was Farmer and it burns me worse than the cut or the trashed shirt—that someone with that kind of money, that kinda house, would have the audacity to be named Farmer.

In tuning her out, somewhere along the trip Meredith has come to this conclusion, "You'll come home with me. That's what will happen. I'll take you home. We'll work this through; come up with a solution."

"Don't get yourself involved, Meredith; you've already done too much."

Ten minutes out of jail, the thought of Meredith taking over as my personal warden already feels suffocating. Only when she turns up Lakeview Drive, Chickawaulkie Pond calm enough to reflect the wooded hills behind it, do I realize the futility of my arguing. She's made up her mind. This is how it will be. She says, "I paid for you to be free, so now I'm in charge, I guess. That's what's best."

My last argument is feeble. It doesn't even sound like an argument when I say, "I need clean clothes."

Apparently, it doesn't sound like an argument to her, either. She tells me she'll run to my house while I clean up. There's no arguing, then. She's decided.

She shows me the bathroom and when she leaves I turn the water on and sit on the toilet, listening to it hiss until the front door slams. I shut the water off.

In the fridge I find a bottle of beer. On her couch, I sit still while a cat explores my personal space cautiously. After testing my lap with her paw, she climbs aboard, curling up to resemble a gag-store plastic-poo and falling to purring. Something about the cat's warm weight holds me in place, so I'm still sitting there with only a sip of beer left when Meredith comes back in.

Glaring at the bottle in my hand, turing her scowl to my greasy hair, she doesn't say anything until she's dropped my wardrobe onto the couch. "That's my beer," she says. "And your house is gross. You should kiss my feet that I was willing to walk in there."

I finish off the beer in a callous swig before telling her, "I didn't ask for that."

"I could have left you in jail."

Pushing the cat off my lap, it lands on the floor with an irritated whine. "It feels like you have." She stands watching me, until

46

I say, "I'm sorry. I'm being an asshole. I know I am. I'm just fucked. And that's not your fault. And I do appreciate the help."

She nods and leaves the room and comes back with two beers. Handing me one, we both have a long sip before she says, "You'll have to sell the house. Quickly."

"I'm not selling the house."

"I don't have any more cash to sink into the Barry fund." She watches me a moment. "Do you even have a job?"

"I've been working with the McKier brothers, out off Buttermilk Lane."

She laughs, a sharp, humorless bark. "The McKier brothers are shut down. Months ago," she says. "The bank took them over. You didn't know that?"

Swallowing twice before pulling the beer from my lips, I manage to drain half the bottle.

She shakes her head. "You're gonna have to sell the house, that's all there is to it."

"No. I've got something else lined up that I can do. An opportunity…"

"An opportunity? Sounds dubious."

"Ajna Canth introduced me to this guy… His daughter's dead, I guess…"

"Oh," she says and we're both quiet. I drink and she watches me, her eyes narrowing before she says, "You can't…"

"Of course not. Of course I can't."

"I don't think I like this, Barry."

"I don't either," I say. "But I don't think I have any options at this point."

"There's always an option. A choice to do right or wrong. Trust me on that, I know: there's always a choice." Standing, she goes into the kitchen behind the couch, pacing there a moment.

47

Her footsteps beat out an aimless loop. Returning, she sits in the lounger across from me and says, "We've known each other... How long, Barry?"

I shrug.

"Right. I was a junior in high school when Ray and I started dating. You were ten. Ray was, like, twenty-four." She shakes her head, muttering, "I still can't believe your father was okay with that. Now, looking back it seems like..."

"I think Pa approved of anyone being in the house if they'd cook..."

Meredith laughs. "Yeah. That sounds about right." Laughing again, awkwardly, she says, "Here's what you don't know about me, Barry: I used to be trouble. I used to shop lift. A lot." She looks away, something dreamy and embarrassing and sensual flitting in her gaze. Wrangling up a severely adult tone, she tells me, "It was a rush. That's why I did it. And I'd steal anything. One time, I stole a pair of boys' jockey shorts, just cause it was there, within reach and I knew I would get away with it. I took them from the general store downtown and threw them away in the first trash can I passed on my way home. The point was getting that rush. It never mattered what I stole." Clearing her throat, she says, "You see, I was always making 'bad' decisions, Barry. Always doing wrong just for that charge, that rush. Ray was the one who got me to stop. I'd had a few close calls—couldn't go into the general store by then, if you know what I mean. Anyhow, I started taking drama classes and, you know what?—I found that same rush was possible, doing something productive. Doing something good..."

"...I remember that production of My Fair Lady. It wasn't good... And, for the record, I didn't break into that house for a fucking rush Meredith. I'm trying to survive here."

Ignoring me she says, "Besides, if you know you can't do what he's offering to pay you for…"

"I don't need to," I say. I've already thought it through, that part anyway. I say, "I just need to convince him that I can. I mean, if he's crazy enough to think that I can summon the dead or commune with them, or whatever it is that he thinks about me, then he's crazy enough to trick into thinking I've done it, right?" I say.

She lets out a slow breath that sounds like the distillate of disappointment before she says, "Do something good, Barry. For a change. Do something good. This is how you start: sell the house and go look for a job—a real one. That way, when you go before the judge you can show…"

"A job? From the job tree?"

"Or the want ads. Whichever."

"It's not that easy."

"It's not that hard, either: you have to try."

"I'm not selling the house. That's the last time I wanna hear about it, because it's not happening, okay? You may as well drop it. As for a real job—I say, what? 'Please hire me: in a few months I'll be going to jail, but please train me and pay me until then. Also, what's your benefits package look like? I'd love full dental.' Does that sound about right? 'Cause no one hires that, Meredith. There aren't any open doors for someone standing where I am."

"What is it with you and that damn house? It's a trailer, for Christ's sake, Barry."

"It's not a trailer; it's my ancestral home. Our ancestral home. Ray's and mine and Pa's and, yeah, yours too. It's our home."

"It looks like a goddamn trailer."

"That's just because it's rundown," I explain.

"It's a curse, Barry. That's what it is. It's the reason you tried robbing that house. If you didn't have the bills to worry over…"

"If I didn't have the house, I wouldn't have anything at all."
She looks at me.

"You see a trailer. That's fine. That isn't what I see—you have to understand that," I take a breath. Turning away from her to a non-point on the ceiling, I say, "I see my father and my brother sitting together, playing cribbage at the dining table." I sigh. "I see the girl from down the street, only a little older than me, trying to be a mom for me out of the kindness…"

"Barry…" she says, cutting me short. "I was trying to act like an adult so Ray would notice me. I think we can both look at that honestly now." Her eyes shift a little as she watches me and we're both quiet. She says, after a moment, "Is any of this illegal?"

"I don't think so."

"I won't do anything illegal, or help you do anything illegal."

"I probably wouldn't ask."

She nods, eyes closed. "I'll help. Okay? I'll help however I can… What's your plan?"

"I don't know. Convince him that I can contact his dead daughter, I guess."

She inhales, breath hissing across her lips.

8

Back in high school, Sarah Goldstein and I were friends. But it's been a long time since high school and when she sees me walk into the lobby of the Rockland Inn, her face turns stiff and cold. Meeting at the reception desk, she tells me in a rigid whisper, "You better not let Canth see you coming in the front door, Cookie..."

"I guess you haven't heard. I've been hired in a professional capacity. So, I'm sure..." I trail off. Turning away, she's given up listening and I follow her gaze beyond the big, dark staircase, to the narrow dining room at my rear. Expecting to find Ajna standing there, instead I find two people who've broken off their conversation to quietly stare at me. Neither one of them is Canth, but the man seated there, I do recognize. Abandoning my conversation with Sarah mid-sentence, I cross to their table.

"Mr. Cook," the man greets me.

I nod down at him and the woman at his side, in turn.

"I don't believe I introduced myself to you properly, the last time we met," he says, offering his hand. "Nevers. Davis Nevers. I'm surprised to see you, Mr. Cook. I suspected we wouldn't meet again." Filling my gap in the conversation, he says, "This is my associate, Priscilla Bloomfield. Priscilla, Mr. Cook."

The woman's in her fifties or sixties, shaped like a lightbulb and has a shock of purple hair topping her head. She smiles and says, "I'm familiar with your reputation, Mr. Cook…"

That word—reputation—gets my face cooking and I stammer a moment, desperately trying to construct an insult to volley back at her; only managing to mutter through my teeth, "Easter egg." It comes out acidic and whispered.

Puzzled by the premature holiday greeting, Priscilla raises her eyebrows to say, "Having saved those vacationers years ago; that man and his daughter."

I exhale. "Right." Nodding nervously I brush the sweat from my forehead.

"Well, good seeing you, again." When I don't move away, Nevers asks, "Was there something in particular you wanted?"

"Yes," I say. I open my mouth once or twice, failing to create any further sound, before I finally manage to make myself say, "Your offer. I'd like to take you up on it…"

"Well. This is a bit awkward. Priscilla happens to be the woman who took the job." Folding his fingers together, he lays the knot of them on the table and affords me a look.

I say, "Her?"

"You weren't interested; it seemed. And Ms. Canth…"

"Well, now I am interested. And I'm…" I can't think of anything to say. After half a moment, I manage, "The man for the job. The man you came for…"

"That may well be, but Priscilla has stepped forward and has proven herself to be… reliable." The word seems lackluster after the long pause but Priscilla smiles anyway.

Stealing one of the unused chairs at the table I plop myself down before either of them can argue against it. Scooting forward, I say, "What are her qualifications? May I ask that? She knows my reputation, said so herself. You know it too. It's what brought you here, right?"

"…Yes and no."

"I have experience here. Documented…"

"No one's arguing that…"

"So," I say, turning to the woman now. "Let me ask: what are your qualifications?"

"We're not in competition, Mr. Cook," she says. I stare at her and, obnoxiously, she straightens, rising to my gaze. "Very well. For starters, I received my Bachelors from Johns Hopkins University; majoring in Neuroscience. After that, I had a bit of a life change, took a few years off before my Doctoral Thesis on Paranormal Psychology. After that I studied shamanism at the Four Winds Center for Contemporary Shamanism in New Mexico. I've since studied Wicca under renowned oracle Christine Evenclaw…"

"So you're a Witch," I say. "You could have just said that without all the fancy bullshit."

She raises her eyebrows.

"'I'm a Witch.' See? That's all you have to say. Simple."

Her face settles into a frown.

I look to Nevers. Laying my hand conspiratorially on his forearm I tell him, "I'm only joking, I hope you understand, when I call her a witch. She has absolutely no supernatural powers at all, I can assure you of that." Turning to her I say, "I, on the other hand…"

By this time Nevers has removed his arm from my touch. I take the occasion to readjust my seat, closer to him so that we're both on one side of the table and Priscilla is relegated to the other, alone. Meanwhile, the Witch's expression has changed again. Following her fresh smile behind me I catch sight of a gaunt, blonde boy crossing the room toward us. "Tomothy," Priscilla announces brightly when the boy takes the seat at her side. His face lights up, smiling at me, saying, "Hello." I give him the finger before returning my attention to Nevers.

"She's a huckster. You know that, right, Nevers? That's why I've come here," I say. I take a deep breath and tell him, "I wasn't gonna help you, but I can't sit by and watch you get grifted by these two carnies."

"I am no huckster. No carny," she says.

"You know how I know you're a fraud? You named this poor, pale whelp Tomothy. Anyone with a snail's depth of intuition could foresee the abuse a child named Tomothy would suffer at the hands of his peers."

"Tomothy is not my son. Tomothy is my apprentice," she says proudly. Turning to him affectionately, laying a hand on his shoulder, she says, "But in many ways he is my teacher."

"Gross. She's humping the child. She's a pervert and a carny."

"I am not 'humping' him. He is a very talented clairvoyant."

"Really?" I say. Turning to him, I ask, "Tell me what I'm thinking right now, Tomothy." When he looks away to Priscilla, I say, "I was thinking Tomothy is the dumbest fucking name I've ever heard." I feel badly, when the boy flinches and turns red. But, I push the guilt away; this is war. He's standing in the way of my goddamned money. He's got his goddamned hand on it.

"If you came here to have fun at our expense, perhaps you should simply leave," Priscilla says.

"I'm not leaving."

"Then I will," she says, looking to Nevers, but making no move to stand.

"Enough," Nevers says. He doesn't say it particularly loudly. But everyone goes quiet. Looking at me, he says, "Why are you here, Mr. Cook? I did understand that you weren't interested in the job, didn't I?"

"I told you... I heard that this con artist had taken you in and that..."

"Nobody's taken me anywhere. And if you're going to waste my time with a bunch of bullshit, you can see yourself out. Or, I can call the management to see you out."

Lowering my voice, I lean in. "I'm in trouble. I'm going to lose my family home: my ancestral home, my birthright. I'll do anything you need. I'll find the ghost, Josephine. And you know I'm the only one who can... But, I need your help."

He leans away, appraising me up and down. "How did you do it last time? How do I know you can do it again?"

Rather than answer, I say, "These two won't find your daughter."

"Will you? Can you? That's the question, Mr. Cook."

"Davis..." the woman starts to say, but he silences her with his palm.

And here is the juncture; the great fork in the path of my life. No is the answer I've always given; the answer I'm comfortable with. But, it is yes that I need. Yes is the bridge forward. Yes is the answer to my problems. The word just won't leave me. Honest, before I can think of a clever way to avoid it, I tell him, "I don't know."

"Davis," the Witch says. "This man is obviously troubled. He's been in and out of jail. And we're making such progress here..."

"It's been slow," he says. "Very slow."

"Yes. I know that you've felt that way, but we're working on a strategy..."

"Nope," he says. His chair scrapes the floor as he stands. Looking down over us all, passing his judgement around, he says, "You said an important word when you said 'competition,' Priscilla. I've made up my mind and I won't hear anymore about it, from either of you. This meeting is over. You're now engaged in a competition. The individual or team who raises my daughter is the one who'll be awarded payment."

"Davis—I beg you to rethink this."

Over Priscilla's protest, I volunteer, "I think you're making a hell of a good call on this one, Nevers. A hell of a good call. That's a shrewd businessman right there. Shrewd. Businessman."

The look he gives me is inscrutable. Reaching into the breast of his coat, he pulls free an envelope and tosses it down on the table before me. It could be anything in there, but I know (every crime movie I've ever seen, tells me) it's a stack of cash. The only mystery being: how deep. "Welcome to the competition," he says and turns and walks away.

Priscilla huffs grandly in his absence. "You've done it now."

"Ruined your mark?"

"Ruined any chance that man has of finding peace."

"Well, you can just call it a day, then."

After Tomothy has helped her up, she says, "I wouldn't give you the satisfaction."

9

Halfway through the lobby, the blonde boy, Tomothy, looks back over his shoulder, offering me a furtive nod-and-grin. Frowning back at him, I bring my hand off the table to flip him the bird, one last time. I keep my seat until the door's shut behind them and they're gone.

Back in the lobby, at the front desk I ask Sarah, "Is Ajna here?"

"Canth is always here," she says, her tone ominous.

"I'm going upstairs to Nevers' room. If you see her, don't tell her that I'm here, okay?"

The expression she makes could be construed as a smile.

I nod and say, "Okay."

I have to knock on Nevers' door three times before I hear his footsteps on the stairs. A moment later his face appears in the gap in the door. Registering no recognition of me he hisses, "What?"

"I was hoping we could speak. Privately."

Grumbling, he steps away, pushing the door wide. Wrapped in a terrycloth robe he lumbers back upstairs to the room and across the room to a pack of cigarettes on the nightstand. He sits on the edge of the bed.

"Ajna hasn't stopped you smoking up the room yet?" I ask.

"You can smoke anywhere you like—in a hospital if you like, in the cancer ward—provided you're willing to pay for it. You aren't here to enforce hotel policy, though."

"I'm not."

"Sit."

I take one of the wicker chairs. It makes me feel awkward, sitting lower than him. His robe is parted over his lap, giving me a much longer view of his inner thigh than I'd like.

"I'm surprised to see you. I figured after you got that advance you'd disappear again."

"So why did you give it to me?"

"Maybe I just wanted to see what you would do. Also, competition can be a powerful business tool, even when it doesn't actually exist." Exhaling, he pours a cascade of smoke right over me. "And, it's true, you said it: you're the one I came for. And here you are."

"Here I am." I look at my hands. "I'll be honest with you, I don't know how to find your daughter."

He nods quietly. "You've come here to tell me this? After taking my money. Bold."

"Well, truth is, I'm not sure how I did it before, either." I look at my hands again. The grooves in my palms are black stained. Dirt that won't wash free. "What I think might help, would be if you told me about her. What kind of girl was she? What was your relationship like?"

"Josephine?" he says, another column of smoke carrying the name into the room. "What does a man ever know of his child?"

I shrug, lift my eyes. "A lot, I would think. But, I don't have children. I wouldn't know."

"You're right. Or, you should be right. The fact is, I wasn't ever a father. Joanne, Josephine's mother, and I divorced when Jo was seven, six or seven. Maybe eight. We lived in Connecticut at the time. We divorced and Joanne did quite well with that. She moved up here with Josephine, bought a house on North Haven Island and that was that, I guess. I saw her," he says, looking to the ceiling and really weighing out his words, "when she was ten, I think. My mother was ill and I had Josephine come down and spend Christmas with my family. I think after that I saw her when she was fifteen, but she didn't have much use for me then; I don't think teenaged girls have much use for fathers, as a rule. But, conjecture—as I've said, I wasn't much of a father to begin with."

"Okay," I say. "I'm confused then, I guess. What are you looking for?"

"My daughter."

"Okay. I guess my question then, is—why?"

He stubs out his cigarette. Stung by smoke, he pinches his eyes closed, rubbing them teary before speaking again, "You must understand, I had a business I worked hard at, a business I started and grew from nothing and it was the center of my life. The very center—the hub of everything I was. I gave myself to it completely, so that there wasn't room left for anything else. Or anyone. Joanne knew that when we married, I told her that—somehow, still, she managed to use it as a weapon against me. Well, that was then. We divorced, she said she was unhappy with the 'emptiness' of our life together. Whatever that means. Her words. It was distressing for me, as you can imagine. It would be for any man, no matter his position. But still, I had the business, my job. I suppose my life didn't change a whole lot. The house was empty when I got home, but that wasn't altogether alien; when we were married I would come home to a sleeping house instead of an empty one," he shrugs. "They're about the same. Only, there's no one to bark at you for making noise. So, I moved on. I dated. Nothing serious, all casual. It was still the business that I was consumed by, that was always the peg I hung my hat on."

With the last one still smoldering in the ashtray, he tugs another cigarette out of the pack before going on. The room isn't very big and I feel like I'm drowning under an ocean of smoke.

"Josephine disappeared—I don't know, she must have been seventeen or eighteen—and Joanne called and was upset and I told her I would help however I could and, in the end didn't help at all, because she didn't call again and the whole thing was, you understand, all the way up here. Miles away. Lives away. You understand." Reading my face for a moment, Nevers says, "What would you have had me do?"

"I don't have children. I don't know the first thing about it. I'm not passing judgement, if that's what you're pissy about."

It takes him a moment to start again. "Honestly, or maybe not, maybe I'm lying to myself when I say this, but I thought, well, she's eighteen and kids go away. They get an itch. They start out on their own and I thought, well, she's just done that. She's just gone, and she'll come back."

"But she never did."

He shrugs. He inspects his cigarette.

"So what did you do?"

"Nothing. I did nothing. She wasn't a part of my life. She never was, so nothing changed. Joanne never called, the offer of help I extended was never taken. Life moved on"

"Okay. Something must have changed. You're here."

"I'm getting to that. I worked for years, maybe a decade after she was gone and—nothing. Nothing at all. An occasional thought about her, I suppose. I would think 'I wonder if she's been found' and then I'd think that I supposed she had been and no one had bothered telling me. Every time I thought of her, that was what I thought: she'd run off, maybe with a boy, and then been found. So I worked. I got up seven days a week and worked for years and then my big payday came. I was offered a price for my business that I would have been a fool to decline. So I took it. After all, that was what I had been in for. You have to understand, my father was an immigrant. He worked in a factory. We were a hand to table family—no stability at all, and that was what I wanted. I wanted solid rock under my feet—polished marble, preferably—not the constantly turning tide my father fought against. So I sold."

"And then?"

"Nothing. And then nothing. The woman I was with at the time, we went out and had champagne and a pricey dinner and I woke to a gray day and a hangover. I finally understood what Joanne meant by 'emptiness.' No ideas in my head to bring into the world. No plans. Nothing. I worried I'd gone deaf, or mad." He laughs and it is joyless. "For all Joanne couldn't take my working, or claimed she couldn't, Deborah couldn't stand my not working. Our relationship soured in weeks and she was gone. I've never been so alone. Or, maybe I had always been just that alone, every bit that alone and hadn't ever noticed. Who can say? That was when the dreams began.

"I started seeing Josephine every night, calling out for my help. I put up with it for months, the nightmares, trying, in the days, to get past them, to forget them. To forget the timbre of her screams. At night I found myself staying up as late as possible, trying to avoid bed, for all I could, trying to avoid the ghost in my dreams, Josephine. Finally, I couldn't take it anymore. I packed my car and started north, thinking she was trying to lead me in, to have me find her and then, there it was again, that emptiness. The silence."

"No more dreams?"

"Precisely."

"Well," I say and shrug. "Maybe you're over it."

Shaking his head gravely, he says, "No. I tried. I drove south again, thinking exactly what you've said, that it was over, just a phase and then over."

"And?"

"The moment I got south of Thomaston the dreams began again. I've stayed in every B&B, motel, hotel and inn in the mid-coast region and I can draw a fault line, nary a mile wide, where the dream exists on one side and not on the other.

"I am a prisoner here. A prisoner until I find a solution and I'm afraid that you, Mr. Cook, may be my best hope. That's something to chew on, isn't it?" he says.

"Yeah," I say. I say, "I think I'm going to need a bigger advance."

That distant look finally washes from his face when he tells me, "Get the hell out of my room."

10

Midmorning, overcast. I haven't been home in two weeks and the house seems to show the vacancy, even though I'm not sure it looks all that different than it did. Off to the side of the driveway, my boat sits on its trailer, the stern full of water and the tongue of the trailer aimed at the sky, the whole rig poised for takeoff; ignorant of the fact that it has no way of getting anywhere now. Not to outer-space, not to the bay. I feel an aching kinship with the boat—without the Dodge, we're both stuck.

It's colder inside than out. I stand in the kitchen a moment, noticing the gray bloom of my breath and the quiet. There's a cold stillness to the room, but the silence is incomplete; a warm layer of static, white noise, charging the air.

It takes me checking beneath the kitchen and bathroom sinks before I open the door to the basement and there, with a choked feeling tightening my guts, the hiss is louder. I don't need to descend into the darkness to know what's happened. The water has risen to the third step, glimmering, black and lapping the wood. The pipes have burst: my long-harbored fear realized.

There's no one to blame for this but myself. And, while I'd rather soak in self-defeat than wade out into the basement, the fact that water's still pouring in drives me to act. Undressing, leaving my clothes in a pile beside the door, I start down, into the cold water. It's thigh high and cluttered with debris. Floating toward me, a canoe paddle tries blocking my path. I push it aside.

The break is in the middle of the pipe, long past the valve. Water sprays from the ceiling. The valve is on the far side of a pile of junk—cherished things turned to junk by stupidity: some of them my father's things, entrusted to me. I drag a heavy guilt as I start fighting through the pile. Trying not to acknowledge the individual artifacts, I toss things aside. It's all just garbage now.

After I get the water shut off, the basement's quiet. It's vaguely satisfying, that silence, until I'm brought back to reality by the lapping of water and the tick-tick-tick of dripping drops. Working my way towards the stairs up to the bulkhead, the sun shines briefly on me when I fling the door open to the day.

I find a five gallon pail, tilted and floating aimlessly, and I start spooning water and tossing it out the door.

"How long was the water running?" I ask.

Ray shrugs. Sitting, his back scooted up against the open bulkhead, the water flies through the air, over him, slapping the ground behind him when it lands. "How should I know?"

When my shoulders start burning with the effort of throwing bucketfuls up the stairwell, I give that up; not in shape for it. Instead, I drown the bucket and hobble up the stairs to dump it out. Panting, on my way back down, I say, "Locked up for a fuckin' week, and you can't stop by and check on things."

"I don't live here, Barry."

"Convenient." My lungs and shoulders burn with the effort. My poor cock and balls, on the other hand, are retreating like they're hoping to work their way into a potentially warmer parallel universe through the duct of my body cavity.

Who knows how long I work. Exhausted, stopping for a break, I sit against the door opposite Ray. Leaning up and opening my throat, I try to catch my breath. The bulkhead is rough and cold. Down at the bottom of the stairs the water table doesn't seem to have receded at all. I swear quietly.

"I don't even want to hear it," Ray says. "None of this is my fault."

I look at him. "It's our house, Ray. Not just mine. I'm..."

"Barry, I told you, you should sell it. Everyone tells you to sell it..."

"Our ancestral home..."

Shaking his head vehemently, he says, "You're the one who calls it that. You're the one who thinks about it like that. No one else gives a shit. Pa moved away, for fuck sakes. He told you to sell it. That's what you're supposed to be doing. Selling it. Look, you're clinging to this." He nods down the stairs, indicating the gaping, lapping pond bound up in our basement. "It's a nightmare. It's a goddamned nightmare."

"Our ancestral home," I say.

"It's a metaphor, is what it is, Barry. A metaphor for the way you cling to things. For the way that what you cling to ruins you."

Steely, turning to him, I say, "Don't let's start that shit again. If I didn't take care of you..."

Standing, walking away from me, he says, "This is how you take care of things."

65

"I was gone, goddamn it."

"That's nobody's fault but your own. I told you not to go into that house."

"You told me you wanted a damn vote!"

"I told you that house wasn't fucking empty! I told you that!"

"Fine," I say. "Fine," I tell him, "You're right, Ray. You're always goddamned right. You wanna see how I take care of things, Ray? I'll goddamn show you."

Lunging back down the stairs, I find my bucket floating near a lally column in the center of the basement. Working anew, reinvigorated by anger, I drown the bucket, fill it, drag it up the stairs, dump it and lurch back down again, determined.

The level of water in the basement drops. I keep going; up and down the stairs mindlessly, almost weightlessly, like a doll yarned about on string.

I don't know if I'm doing all the work. Maybe Ray is taking bucket loads of his own through some other exit—up the stairs into the house, dumping them out in the bathtub. Or, maybe the water's leeching out through a hidden crack somewhere. I can't say for sure, but soon my bucket's scraping the floor when I dunk it.

There's still some left—an undulating glaze, some inches deep —when I throw out my last bucket to sit on the top stair, watching down into the darkness. Ray is gone. I have no idea how long ago he left, but I feel vindicated: having taken care of my mess. The triumph is hollow, though, with no witness; with no one to hear me gloat.

My feet feel like blocks of wood, only vaguely in league with my legs as I hurry to the bathroom; the waning day like a battery burning down. I dry myself with an off-smelling towel and I climb back into my clothes. In my bedroom, I pack up a bag. I can't help how packing feels—like I'm heading away on a long trip, maybe leaving forever, even though I'm only going down the road some miles to Meredith's house. From the night stand I collect my wad of cash—Ajna's cash for the lobsters, the twenty she gave me to follow her upstairs.

Nevers' manilla envelope full of bills is still in my pocket and I dig it out, folding all the money in together before tucking the envelope back into my jacket.

Outside, nighttime is covering up the world.

I hobble like a man unaccustomed to walking as I start out, onto the street.

11

Stumbling, dirty and disheveled, walking backward into the darkness of night with my thumb out, I'm picked up by an old man in a rusty Coupe Deville. In the perfunctory halo of the dome light, the dog laid out on the backseat looks dead. It's only after I've climbed in and the light has shut off that I feel the dog nuzzle my shoulder. He breaths deeply for a moment and falls back, as though disappointed by what he found.

The old man starts the car forward and, back on the road a moment, he asks, "You're Barry Cook. Work with them McKier boys—don't you?"

"That's right. Did, anyways. They went under, I guess…"

"You mightn't remember me. Emmet Thompson. I was a friend of your father's. Something of a friend, more or less."

"Is that right?" I nod into the dark, ensuing silence in the cab.

"Acquaintance, might be a better word."

"I'll say 'hi' to him for ya."

"He might not be happy you mentioned me. I don't think he ever cared for me all that much." The old man coughs and we go silent. "Where you headed?"

"Off Lake View."

"We old-timers call that Route Seventeen."

"That so?" I ask, and then I ask, "Should you be driving?" because he's let the car drift over the center line—settled now, snuggly into the oncoming lane. I hold tight to the door handle and, gradually, the car meanders back where it belongs.

"Where you say you were going?"

"Lake View," I tell him again.

"I'm only going to downtown."

"That'll be fine. In fact, if you wanna let me out here..."

"—Barry Cook, right?"

"That's right."

"I remember. You findin' your brother and that man and his daughter... Can't remember their names... Andrews. Paul, was it? What was his girl's name?"

"I don't know, that wasn't me," I tell him. "That was somebody else you're thinking of."

"It gave everybody a lot of hope, that. Made people think that God really was watching over us, taking care of us. Some of us anyways; some of the time. Your brother was a good boy," he says. Turning to look at me, the car leaves the traveling lane again, this time in favor of the break down lane. When he looks back up, he seems oblivious to the change and we travel in the breakdown lane for awhile, the right tire occasionally dipping and sucked off into the soft shoulder.

"I think you've confused me with someone else," I say, bracing myself against the door and the dash.

He checks the mirror and the shoulder sucks the wheel in and, with the whole vehicle quaking, the old man wrestles to get the car back up. Fearing he hasn't the strength, I reach out, grab the wheel and help him push. When the car humps back on the road, I'm covered in sweat.

Between the cranking heater and the constantly escalating fear for my life, I'm itching for the cold night air as the car approaches the Burger House on the edge of downtown Rockland.

"Right here," I say.

He cruises past the Burger House and then by Route Seventeen and I say, "Right here, Emmet, is good. Why don't you let me out right here?"

I catch glimpses of his face in the wash of streetlights whipping past. His eyes are trained, dully on the road. Looking back, Route Seventeen is gone from sight as he comes around the corner and passes through the yield sign that divides Main Street and Union Street, taking the turn too fast, crossing over the line with the tires starting to shriek.

"Anywhere here is good, Emmet," I tell him. He keeps staring ahead, blinking at the road. His hands are locked at ten and two and he takes the turns with his shoulders. I look back again, the distance to Meredith's house—only minutes ago shrinking and shrinking—is growing longer again. "Right here," I say as he cruises by the Rockland Public Library and then I say it again, louder—I'm just about yelling now—when he passes the Court House.

I've nearly given up asking when he pulls up in front of the Rockland Inn and turns to me and says, "Well, here you are."

I clear my throat. "Yup. I guess I am."

"It was nice seeing you again, Barry Cook. It's a good omen, my seeing you. I always take it as that."

"I'm not..." I start to say, but the words dry up before I get them out. "Keep an eye on that centerline," I tell him. He winks at me—it looks epileptic—as I pull my duffel bag free and shut the door.

His tail lights drift off around the corner and gone. I heft up my bag, about to turn back down the street when a Prius parked in front of the Inn catches my attention.

12

Maybe it's the lack of other cars along the road. Maybe it's the Prius's strangely familiar shade of purple. Whatever it is, some unaccountable gravity draws me right to it. Circling the sedan, I find the rear bumper, the hatchback and a good swath of the back window are plastered over with bumper stickers, the least kitschy of which is one for Johns Hopkins University. The others are along these lines: Honor the Goddess, My other ride is a Broom, Tarot Readers do it on the Table. Ugh.

My jaw locks up. I'm certain it's hers. The Witch. Coming around the grille I'm seized by an urge to clobber in the headlamp with my boot heel. The itch of working over those lights and leaving them in shards is almost more than I can bear and my foot's already off the ground when a voice from behind freezes me up. "What's up, kin?"

I drop the foot. Almost tripping over myself, shamefaced, I hop back up onto the sidewalk.

"Jeez, didn't mean to catch you off guard, Cookie."

In a darkened corner of the Rockland Inn's covered porch, a cigarette ember throbs brightly for a moment. Muttering into the darkness, I say, "Don't call me Cookie."

As he steps forward, into the cast of the streetlight, I recognize the boy's face, if only vaguely. Looks a little like my brother, truth be told. The cluelessness at his name must register openly on my face. He quickly says, "Drew."

I nod. "Right. Drew." I still can't quite place him.

"I worked for the McKier's with you last summer. Place off Buttermilk."

"Yeah. That's right." I nod now, more confidently.

"We worked on Fifty Eight Summit, before that. You remember that?" Drew says. Fingering a little blemish of whiskers on his chin he says, "You probably didn't recognize me with the goat. It's coming in pretty thick."

"Sure."

"How you been?"

"Gettin' by," I say, stepping away, turning my shoulder to him, a clock-tick toward my back coming around.

"Heard you'd gone into county."

I stop, shaking my head. "That was someone else."

Down off the porch now, halfway down the stairs, the stark glare of the streetlight flares flatly off his hand and the high points of his face. He nods toward the street.

"You got an itch over that Prius, or what?"

"The fuck you talking about," I say. The more I hear from the kid, the more I remember him. He was always hanging on, talking to talk; taking both ends of an argument. After a few days working with him, I got in the habit of running my circular saw the moment I saw him turn a corner.

"You're just eyeballing it," he says. "Makes me wonder—what's with the Prius, kin?"

"I don't know. What's with the Prius?"

He shrugs. "Pricey car to be throwing a bunch of stickers on."

"Hippies," I say.

He nods. "You shoulda seen the nut that climbed out of it."

"Purple hair? I've seen her."

"Creepy little kid with her, too. Blonde as sunlight and looked about as heavy."

"When did they go in?"

Smiling big and talking proudly, he says, "See? I knew it. I knew you were eyeballing it. I knew you were curious the way I saw you..." A cold-eye's all it takes to shut him up. He says, "Five minutes ago. Couldn't have been longer. I'd just lit my smoke." He looks at the cigarette, which has burned down to nothing. Pitching it toward the street, the butt and it's ember come uncoupled in the air.

"Thanks," I say. Throwing my bag up onto the landing behind him, I say, "Have another cigarette and watch my bag a minute."

"Cookie, I gotta..." he starts saying, but I've already passed him and pushed open the door to the lobby and it winds shut behind me, cutting him off quiet.

Sarah Goldstein's at the front desk again, a smile briefly flitting on her face, before our eyes meet and her look goes bland. "If Canth knows you've been using the front door..."

"I told you, that's all set. Is the Witch with Nevers or is she here with Ajna?"

"What are you talking about, Cookie? You better get moving along before..."

"Don't call me... Listen, I'm working on a big job right now," I say, lowering my tone shrewdly. "I could use a hand. Can I trust you, Sarah?"

The frown that's settled on her face doesn't loosen.

"What I'm saying is that there's money and work to go around. I'd like it if I could trust you to be my eyes and ears around here. Nothing that'll interfere with your regular duties, just, you know, keeping me abreast of Nevers' comings and goings, who comes to see him—that sort of thing. What'd you say?"

She blinks. "Whatever."

"Thanks, Sarah. It'll be worth your while. Do me a favor. Call up to Nevers' room and tell him... Tell him I got a big break—something important I need to see him about. Tell him it's urgent..."

She appraises me silently for a moment before picking up the phone and stabbing a few buttons, her eyes dully fixed on mine. "Barry Cook's here," she says and she hangs up and nods me toward the stairs.

"Once again, Sarah—I appreciate you keeping my being here between the two of us. There's no need for Ajna to know about this. And, Sarah?—thanks."

She blinks at me again. "Whatever."

I head up the stairs.

Crossing down the long hallway, voices drone from beyond Nevers' door and I'm only just starting to raise my fist to knock, when the door beside me yawns open and I turn.

Ajna's waiting, unperturbed, unimpressed—bored with my persistent existence—inside the room to my right. "Come in," she says. "Close the door."

My face is suddenly flush; realizing I have all my money—every last damned penny—in that manilla envelope in my pocket. Something inside me is begging me to turn, to run, to just bolt down the stairs. It's too late. I step into the room and close the door.

"Sit," she instructs, but the room is much smaller than Nevers' and only holds the bed, which she's already taken, and two night stands. Still, that she's commanded means I must comply. I grunt, lowering myself to sit on the floor. Looking up at her, I feel like a little kid. She smiles. "Barry," she says. "What did I tell you?"

"Only Ajna sticks up for Barry?" I say, working a smile on my face.

She has no smile to return. "You've tried to cheat me, Barry."

"No," I say. "I wouldn't, Ajna. You know I wouldn't."

"So you didn't tell Sarah to keep quiet about your being here, the other night? About your going up to Nevers' room? Curious. I wonder why she would fabricate such things. Can you imagine why, Barry?"

"Maybe you have an employee who's lying to you."

Now she shows me a smile. "I suspect you're right. There's a penalty, you understand?"

"I don't have it with me," I tell her.

The smile deepens. Her eyes narrow. "Explain to me. How a crook like you gets by, being such a poor liar." Her eyes fall on the bulging pocket of my jacket.

"How much do you want?"

"What is fair?" she looks to the ceiling. Figuring it in her brain, before turning back to me, she shrugs. "If you had payed me to begin with I would have only asked for half. Now, I'm afraid, I must insist on it all. As a matter of principle, you understand."

"All of it?" I say, stammering. I manage to make myself say, "Seventy-five dollars?"

"More than that. Much more. A brown envelope full of cash. Sarah has told me of it."

"I'll give you a hundred dollars."

She wags a finger at me. "No, no. That is not fair. You're missing the principle entirely. You tried to cheat me. You violated our agreement. How could I possibly let you leave with anything? You wouldn't learn the lesson. You would be taught nothing. Even if you hadn't cheated Ajna, I could not possibly let you grift my guests for so paltry a sum."

"Grift? You were the one who set this all up..."

"You remember wrong. I have nothing to do with any of this. I am the matchmaker. An individual seeks another and I help foster the connection. Yes? Had you not cheated me, that service alone would be worth half your earnings. Where would you have found employ, if not for Ajna?" When she says her name she touches her chest, as though she's worried I'll confuse who she's talking about. She finishes, saying, "And the risks she takes."

"I'm the one providing the services."

"And I am your pimp. Whores need pimps. Protection. Yes? You cannot pass into my hotel for less than the whole envelope. It is fair."

I shake my head. "I thought you were a matchmaker."

"I feel as though I'm not being understood. You cannot leave my hotel for less than the whole envelope. You have tried to cheat me. I'll have all of it," she says. "All of it now and your assurance that you won't try to cheat me again in the future." Her declaration of the word 'future' is accented by the crisp click of a switchblade opening. Displaying the narrow knife-blade, she works the reflection from it to glare in my eyes.

I flinch from the light. "You can't take my money."

"I am taking what is owed to me."

I start to rise, but when she flicks the blade again, I slump back on my ass. After a strained moment I manage to make myself say, "You can't kill me."

"Can't." She smiles, echoes the word, "Kill," and holds my gaze a moment. "You are special, Barry, you know that? People have forgotten with time—you have forgotten. But I know. I will not forget. Your fear of me proves it. Taller than me, nearly twice, heavier than me, four fold—still you know enough to cower in light of my gaze. You know," she says. She leans forward, "You know, more than anyone, what I've done. What I am still capable of. Look at me," she says. I have not turned away. I find I can't. "Tell me what it is you see in my soul. What I know you see there..."

I shake my head. An opaque catalogue of atrocities is written on her—so thick and dark, she almost can't be seen beneath. Anyone can see that. I tell her, "You're wrong."

"Stand and leave," she indicates the door at my back with the point of her knife. But I don't stand. I don't leave. I cannot. She'll bury that knife in me if I try. "No? Perhaps then..." she raises her head, offering her neck and when I still don't budge she looks at me, sadly. Her posture relaxes and she says, "And yet you know, Barry. You know I am no monster. You know I am simply a product of desperate circumstance." Still staring at me, her eyes start to twitter, pools thickening in the basins. "You know what I have done. What I have sacrificed, what I still have to sacrifice. What I will still do, if provoked."

"I'm just asking to keep what's mine."

She shakes her head. "I would have nothing. You would allow me nothing. The world will not give, to me, anything. Never. I must take, or accept nothing. That is always the way. Maybe not for everyone, but it is my curse. And you know."

"You're not big enough to drag me to the dumpster. You're not big enough to drag me two feet."

"The Jew, Goldstein, could help, I'm sure."

My voice trembles unconvincingly when I say, "We're friends."

She shakes her head, clicks her tongue, testing out a quick rhythm. "She is no friend to you, Barry. You're quite blind for someone who sees so much."

I say, "She doesn't have the stomach for it."

"It may be you're underestimating her disdain for you. But, perhaps you're right. We both know you're right, I suppose. About her. She is weak. About my being too small. In that sense, I too am weak. You're right." Her smile gets tighter as she slips off the bed, the light reflecting off the knife making me flinch again. "But who would bother hiding your body when you came in here, crazed and threatening? No matter what I will do to you, rest assured, it will only be in self defense. But you don't need to hear me say it. You know. You know I will not let you leave with a penny. You've already given me what I demand. Already in your mind, you've submitted it to me."

I take the envelope from my pocket and hand it over.

Collecting her money, she smiles. Patting me on the head, she says, "You're a good boy. Who knows, maybe we can salvage this business relationship."

13

"I'm not buying you fast food, Barry—we just ate," Meredith says.

"We did?"

"I made you a salad. What happened to all your cash, anyway?" When I'm silent, she says, "Barry? What happened to all that money?"

The first lie I can think of is the one that falls out of my mouth. "I paid the electric bill."

It sounds like she might deflate entirely, when she sighs and says, "What a waste. You need a lawyer and, instead, you're wasting money on that decaying shack. I should have left you in jail." She should be watching the road, but she's looking at me and shaking her head. I don't respond. Finally she looks away, attending to the car's operational needs—accelerating out of the parking spot she's established in the middle of the street.

It's just barely drizzling, gray outside and the windshield wipers plow back and forth, farting over the half-dry glass as she turns off onto a side road, coming up a long gravel lane that cuts between a couple of houses into the rutted eastern entrance of the Achorn Cemetery.

"I'm not asking for oysters. I'm not asking for a damn porter house. Burger House is... Like they're practically giving the shit away."

"First of all, shit is right. Do you know what that stuff does to your colon? After we get done here, I'll make you something back at the house."

"Is it gonna be another salad?"

"Are you criticizing what I'm feeding you, Barry? Just so we're clear—is that what you're doing? I'm giving you a bed, food, beer, which, as an aside, I really shouldn't be. I'm driving your car-less-butt around, engaged in this dumb scheme that I should know a-hundred-percent-better than to get involved in, in the first place."

I let a moment pass before saying softly, "So no Burger House?"

She gives up words, growling lightly and parking the car. The cemetery stretches away from us as though in accord with history—older and older in the distance and fainter and fainter through veils of rain and mist. "Haven't been here in a while," she says quietly.

We climb out into the dreary day and I wait by the car while she crosses down a row, an umbrella in one fist and a torch of flowers in the other. I look away while she bends down, leaning the bouquet up against a headstone. "Do you wanna..."

"No, I'm good," I say. "Good."

After a few moments she comes back and we start between the rows, Meredith watching to the left while I watch to the right; anonymous names and arbitrary dates sifting by.

We've marched through some half-dozen rows before she says, "I thought you said it was around here." Having stopped, I take the opportunity to slip in beside her, beneath the umbrella and she readjusts to give me some space. The rain, thin as it is, has driven the cold right into me.

I tell her, "I don't know, exactly."

Blinking theatrically—a practiced face from her years as an aspiring actress—she shakes her head. "It could be anywhere in here?" The cemetery extends impossibly wide around us, bone colored obelisks holding up the low, distant sky.

I say, "Or some other cemetery, I guess. Actually, it might make more sense if she was in another cemetery. Buried on North Haven, probably."

That theatrical blinking, if it can be imagined, becomes even more exaggerated as Meredith continues looking at me. "I'm soaking wet," she says.

"You're not as wet as I am. You have an umbrella."

"What the heck did you bring me out here for, Barry?"

"I don't know." Looking around the cemetery, there isn't anyone here but us. It's dreary and gray—who else would come out on a day like this? "I guess... I don't know. Maybe, I thought she'd show up here."

In spite of the cold, Meredith's face has taken on a ruddy, reddish tone. Shaking her head, she says, "I'm at a loss, Barry. Are you thinking you're going to find a ghost here? Is that what this is?"

"I don't know. Seems like a good place for one." I smile. I open my arms to indicate the day. "Perfect weather for one."

"...'Cause I thought we were just pretending and, I don't know if you're aware of this, but we can pretend pretty darn good from indoors. From my couch, even. Out of the rain. You see what I'm getting at?"

Ray is out in the rows. Moving away and then close again, weaving a line between the columns of markers. His head's down and he's dark in the distance, but I can tell at a glance that it's him.

"Barry?"

"Yeah?"

"Why are we here?"

"This might not make sense to you, but I feel I may be more convincing for Nevers if I'm a little convinced myself. So, you see, it doesn't really matter if she's buried here, or somewhere else, or not buried at all—not even dead, for that matter—what matters is that I convince myself. You know, that I think I'm trying to find her."

"This is your plan."

"It's the best I've come up with so far," I say. "But, I'm open to suggestions."

"Great. Great. Thanks." Meredith turns and starts off.

"Where are you..."

"Back to the car, Barry. Come along whenever you're..." She gestures with her free hand but doesn't complete the thought. The umbrella bobs off down the rows and I turn out into the graveyard to find Ray, retreating beyond the row of barren trees and I can see, a little clearer now, that he isn't just pacing, he's waving me down, inviting me to follow.

Passing through a partition of hedges, I come out into the greater breadth of the cemetery. Old stone, ornate and modest both, clutter the land, polished and gleaming with rain. Ray waits for me beneath a twisted oak near the back of the graveyard. Collecting and sloughing water with its big, bony arms, the weather seems worse in the tree's shade. Big bulbs of rain patter the ground and my shoulders, run through my hair like slithering things.

In Ray's eyes, there's an empty look that I don't like, an uncharacteristic seriousness that I'd rather not face. And his voice is grave and unfamiliar when he says, "Tell me where you want me to take you."

"I don't know what you're getting at, bud," I say, my voice frail.

"Yes. You do. Tell me what you want." He turns, pointing out across the cemetery, across the gray forest at its edge. "She's out there. Waiting. But, I need to know if you want to find her—if that's what you want."

I close my eyes. It fills me with dread, this way he's acting. It's been a long time, since I last saw that gray tempest in his eyes. Back then I was still a child, twelve, and I followed him. Because I didn't know any better, I followed him down to the water and out to sea and... Now, I know better. The thought of finding again, anything like what I found back then, nearly buckles my knees. "No," I say, shaking my head. "I don't want to find her. I don't want to see. I don't want to know."

His hand on my shoulder is gentle but heavy. He looks at me, his gray eyes deep and spiraling.

Stepping away from his touch, still shaking my head, I tell him, "No, Ray. I can't do it again. I wish I'd never done it the first time."

Still, that gray discordance sits in his gaze, even as his voice has taken on some empathy. "You saved them and now you work so hard to forget their names. To pretend you never knew their names at all. To pretend you weren't the man who saved them. To pretend you don't have the power to be that man again…"

"I wasn't a man, is the thing. I was a fucking kid," I say. "And fuck them. I saved them? I couldn't get you to listen to me. You or Pa. That was the reason they needed saving in the first place. The answer's no, Ray. I don't want answers. I want to pretend; that's all I want. I don't even want that. I want as little as it takes to get through this job…"

"Then Meredith was right. You didn't need to come here."

"Is she here?" I ask, almost choking on the words. "Josephine?"

That silvery vacuity in his look fades. He smiles as though he didn't hear me. "Let's go back," he says, smiling as though he's forgotten everything.

I nod and follow him back through the cemetery, back to where Meredith's car waits, hidden by the rise of the earth. I have, as I walk, the eery itch of being watched. Even without turning, I know what she'll look like. I stare at Ray's back as he glides and swaggers amongst the gravestones, but I can see Josephine behind me, clear as a photograph. I can see her waiting on the dark edge of the woods, watching me shirk away. I'm a coward and it makes me feel sick, being in my own skin, knowing that I'm leaving her lost and in need of finding.

Pausing at the break of hedges, there's nothing there, no one waiting at the line of the forest when I do turn back. Ray's probably wrong, at any rate. How could he know where she is, who she is, at all? He's moved on anyway, asking, "Did I ever tell you about Sharon Wickworth?"

For once, I find myself not tuning Ray out as we cut the remaining distance to the car. There's something pleasant in his dumb stories, something that drives off the cold of the rain. Still, I must have some leaden look on my face when I slide back in beside Meredith.

"Jesus, Barry. You okay? You look like you've seen a..." She stops herself and snorts to stifle a laugh. "Sorry."

The cab's so hot I can smell the insides of my nostrils cooking. She hands me a towel from the back seat and I dry my face and my hair and before I'm done we're back out on the road, headed toward downtown Rockland.

"Whatever you want," she tells me when she pulls into the Burger House parking lot.

Sitting at a little round table by the window, the restaurant's warm enough so that the day outside might seem like something on TV, if it weren't woven into my clothes. As I'm cramming down the last of my fries, she says, suddenly, earnestly, but almost at a whisper, "I'm not a bitch."

"I didn't say you were a bitch."

"Well, I'm not."

"No one said that."

"Good."

14

The house is quiet after Meredith's left for work. I flounder on the couch awhile, unable to settle into doing anything; there's no cable and her books are boring. The cat has claimed territory, curled into a ball on the windowsill. It stirs, watching me suspiciously when I rise to go to the door.

Beyond the shade of Meredith's little, wooded lot, the sun glares down without warmth. Out onto the road, I start toward downtown Rockland. "I'd really prefer it," Ray tells me, "if you wouldn't drag Meredith into this."

"I'm not dragging her…"

"It's just… She gets carried away with stuff, you know? The story about her being a shoplifter, that was no joke. And she…"

I grumble, "And I can do with fewer committees, I think." Turning, I throw my thumb out when a car approaches from behind. The driver never once looks at me—an expression of strained indifference tightening his face as he narrows his eye to the road.

After the car's gone and I've spun back around and we've resumed our walking pace, Ray says, "Did I ever tell you about Suzy Trask? She had these huge areoles. No boobs on the girl, mind you…" Another car approaches, and I turn my thumb out again.

"They looked kinda like how you draw eyes on a smiley face. Just round, you know. Perfectly round. Like surprised eyes. Like those areoles were shocked as shit to end up somewhere where there weren't any boobs at all…"

Only after the car's passed and I've turned back, marching forward again, do I cut him off, "Ray! I don't care! I don't care about Suzy Trask's giant fucking nipples. I don't care. I don't want to hear about it."

After a moment, he says, "The nipples weren't big. Just the areoles." I give up trying to thumb. Quiet, we continue along, pushed occasionally by the quick gusts that accompany passing cars. After some silence, he says, "What else is there to talk about?"

"Everything," I say. "Everything, Ray."

"After a man is dead and gone, Barry—let's say some captain of industry, some real loaded self-important twat, buried deep in the ground—what do you think he's longing for, Barry? The millions? The cars? The private jet? The booze? No. I'll tell you—it's ladies. Because, in the end, that's what this whole human comedy is couched on: screwing. Without sex there's none of us and, let's be honest, without, at the very least, the potential of sex none of us would want to keep rolling out of bed in the morning, anyway. So, there's nothing else worth taking time to think about, nothing else worth wasting breath talkin' about…"

"There's everything to talk about, Ray. Everything. Popular culture…"

"First off, what do either of us know about popular culture?"

"A lot," I say. "I know a lot about popular culture."

"When was the last time you bought an album? Do they even make albums anymore?"

"Of course they make albums." There's a cold wind coming over Chiakawaukie pond, and I turn my collar up against it. "Dire Straits. *Brothers in Arms*," I say. "That's a great fucking album."

"*Money for Nothing*? Sure, it's a great album, Barry. It came out in 1985. And you're telling me you think we're qualified to have a discussion about popular culture? Come on, man."

"I didn't buy it in 1985."

"Regardless of when you bought it, it still came out in 1985 and probably hasn't been considered culturally relevant since, oh, 1986 or so... Not to mention—not to mention!—that Brother's in Arms, when it's all said and done is just a recording—and I'm not saying a 'record' here, mind you—but, a recording of the efforts of Mark Knopfler and three other dudes to get some ass. You ever consider how much a guitar looks like a cock, dude? That's all a guitarist is doing, stroking a big phallus, so that ladies will look his way."

"It makes music, too, Ray."

"A bass looks like an even bigger, giant cock. The drummer? What's he hitting those skins with? Two little dicks. You ever seen a drum stick up close? It doesn't so much look like a little dick as it is a little dick. And you listen to the mix, dude: bass is always quietest, right? Bassists' got the biggest dick. He doesn't need to be all loud about it. Drums? Loudest instrument. Little dicks. See what I'm saying..."

I shake my head. "What's the point of this?"

"You're just going to have to admit it, women are the only thing worth talking about. In the culmination of a man's life, they're all that's worth thinking about. And you're only mad because you don't have anything to contribute to the conversation. That's all this boils down to."

"Conversation? You're calling this conversation?"

"What's really sad, Barry—that you're not even seeing—is that when you die all you're gonna think about is how much of your life you wasted just not..."

"That's bullshit, Ray. I've done tons of stuff."

"Name a girl you laid."

"It's not all about that..." In spite of the cold wind, my face has grown hot. I say, "Sarah Goldstein," spitting the name out like it's a mouthful of vinegar.

"Sarah Goldstein? Sarah Goldstein. That fat girl from your senior year home room?"

"She wasn't fat."

"She was enormous. But, that's beside the point." He settles to nodding, thoughtfully. "Okay, Don Juan, tell me about it. Tell me all about Sarah Goldstein."

"Just because you're crass and can't think of anything else to talk about..."

"I'm crass?" Ray says, "You're jealous of my conquests."

"Conquests? There's like, five ladies you talk about, Ray. Like ten stories you tell over and over. Besides, maybe I'd have a chance to have a little fun of my own if I wasn't always stuck taking care of you."

Ray coughs out a quick laugh. "Taking care of me. Taking care of me? That's rich. Wake up, Barry. I'm taking care of you. That's what I do. That's why I'm here, right now and always, because Barry can't hold his own. You can't keep a job. You're barely keeping a handle on the house..."

"Fuck you. All you do is talk. Talk about this girl and that girl and you never once talk about Meredith. It's like you're not thinking about her at all. You talk about taking care of me! Where would you be without Meredith? Wake up, fuck head. You'd be freezing your ass off in Dad's house right beside me."

"Don't bring Meredith into this." We've both stopped, face to face. Behind us, beyond the pavement, Chiakwaulkie pond is gray and choppy.

"Everyone knows it Ray, how you take advantage of her."

"By everyone, I assume you mean yourself. I guess I need to remind you who's couch you're sleeping on. Who's beer you're drinking."

"What the fuck's that supposed to mean?"

"Maybe it's time I moved on. Maybe you're right. Maybe you'd be better off alone," he says and after a moment, nose to nose, he lets go of his breath and turns away. I wish that I hadn't left the house. My nose and cheeks are cold and the world out here feels, suddenly, very lonely.

15

The shops on Main Street have their flags out, swaying in the cold, bright day. Though the roadway is busy enough, the street-side parking is mostly empty—a sure sign of the progress of the season. Winter is coming: that's Autumn's message—pronounced sharply enough now to keep most people away—get used to the cold, diminishing days; it will only get worse. I think about that and try to put my approaching prison stay in perspective. Huddling my jacket around myself I think, I won't have to walk down this blistery, cold road when I'm locked up. Nope. There'll be none of this. It's the sourest comfort you could summon. It's no comfort at all.

Passing the general store, the front window plastered with t-shirts and bits of nautical bullshit—I'm reminded of Meredith's story about stealing jockey shorts—I chuckle to myself and keep moving. I pass by the Electric Company. The bartender inside's wiping the bar-top down; the place is empty. After another block, I finally stop. Over the storefront before me the wide sign reads, 'Priscilla's Magic Emporium.' On the door a second, smaller, handwritten sign says, *Palm and Tarot readings on request; can tell your future, past, find lost love. Walk-ins welcome.*

Accepting the invitation, I push inside.

A bell chimes and when the door closes behind me, I stand, just inside the entrance a moment—listening. Water gurgles in a fountain in the corner. Scents of lavender and vanilla crowd the place, so pungent I can feel the weight of them on my tongue.

The room is divided by shelves laden with mystic bric-a-brac and various bits of dorkery: statuettes of wizards holding cut-glass orbs, displays of incense, crystal balls, medallions and trinkets—metric tons of useless bullshit. Seated buddhas and dreamy cement angels crowd the floor. The sales counter is empty but, from a back corner, Priscilla's disembodied voice chimes, "I'm back here. Please come around if you need anything."

At the back of the store, in an alcove made half-private by a hanging tapestry, I find two pairs of shoes facing off beneath the fringe. It's Nevers, one of those pair of feet is, I'd wager—encased in glimmering patent leather. I'm so certain it's him I don't even pause to think before throwing the curtain wide and announcing, "Ah-Ha!"

Nevers is not there. Instead I find Tomothy (the plasticky shoes are his) and Priscilla, startled in the moment I catch them. The tapestry, hung at the corners, swings right back, cutting us off again. With a clumsy back-step, I bump up into a shelving unit, the trinkets collected on it chattering. By the time I've steadied it, Priscilla has emerged from the alcove. "Ah-ha?"

"I thought Nevers was here," I say.

"Well, as you can see, he is not." Her gaze wanders away, just beyond my left shoulder. Turning to follow her line of sight, I find nothing behind me. But Priscilla says, "Ah! A guest! Come in... Please come forward... Aren't you exquisite!"

Looking back, over my shoulder again, I half-expect to find Ray there, waiting just behind me. But, again, there's no one there at all. No Ray. No one.

Pinning the tapestry up to the wall, Priscilla exposes the little alcove so I can see the table in there, a big glass orb in a fancy stand in the center and, splayed around it, a deck of colorful cards. There, too, is Tomothy, not so little or young as he first seemed—he must be in his twenties, but that tow-head hair and parchment-skin makes him seem child-like at a glance. Childlike or dead, or a combination of the two.

"Tomothy, go get a bowl of water, please," Priscilla instructs, once the curtain is set aside.

Nodding and standing, he disappears through a door at the back of the alcove while Priscilla retakes her seat. Ignoring me, she settles in, staring at the wall opposite her.

"I have business to discuss with you," I say.

Without bothering to give me a glance, she shushes me. "I'm not interested in you, *yeller*. I want to visit with our esteemed guest here." Turning back to the wall, she mutters, "Is he always so loud? So clumsy?" After a pause, she laughs at nothing, inclining her head to the ceiling. "He is a bit like a drummer isn't he? A lot of noise and not much else." She laughs again.

In the meantime, Tomothy has returned with a serving bowl full of water, which he struggles to keep from spilling as he sets it on the tabletop. Seating himself, the two go about an exaggerated business of ignoring me by means of staring at approximately the same spot on the wall, nodding and gesticulating as though someone were speaking, which is highly obnoxious to watch as someone who actually wants to be heard. I shout, "Hey!"

It gets Priscilla's attention. She turns to me, her face twisted up in annoyance. "What?!"

"I need to speak with you. About some business."

"We're busy. We're busy discussing important matters," she nods to the wall, "With our esteemed guest. If you would like to speak, you can go wait out front and I will make time for you when we are done. Is that clear enough?"

"You're going to speak with me now. Or, I'm gonna smash up every last J.R.R. Tolkien-looking-piece-of-shit in your god-damned shop. You understand? I'm not asking to be heard. I'm telling you straight-god-damned-up we have business to discuss."

Raising her eyebrows, she crouches forward out of her chair, picking it up off the floor. Turning it to face me, she drops it so the legs clatter down and she dumps her body back into it, facing me with crossed arms. "Well?"

"Right," I say and clear my throat. "I just want you to know that Nevers is my client, not yours. So, keep your patchouli candles and bullshit away. Consider yourself warned."

She nods. "Is that so?"

"Yeah," I say. "That's so."

Leaning in, lowering her voice, she tells me, "If you feel your client should be seeing you exclusively, that is an issue, I suggest, that you take up with your client. Are we clear?"

I shake my head. "I'm not asking for you to stay away. I'm fucking telling you."

"So it's a threat, then?"

"A warning."

She takes a breath. "Now here's your warning: if you don't leave peaceably and this very instant, I will call the police and I will have you charged with trespass and criminal threatening."

"I think we understand each other," I announce boldly and turn to the door.

In the alley beside the 'Emporium,' I find the purple Prius and go around to the front of the hood and, lifting my boot high, proceed to bash the ever-living-hell out of the passenger-side head-light. Stomping until it goes to shards, I keep kicking until I'm drooling with the absent-minded oblivion of destruction and I feel a hand land on my shoulder, turning me around. I already have my fist cocked back when I lay eyes on Ray's face. "What the hell are you doing?"

A pedestrian has crossed in front of the alley, fixing me with a long frown. I drop my head and let Ray usher me through to the opposite street-side, my face hot with guilt.

"You're gonna get yourself arrested," he tells me.

"What am I supposed to do, Ray? This is, like, the last chance I get here and I got nothing. That Witch and her albino boy-toy are gonna walk off with my payday and what the fuck can I do to stop 'em?"

"So you were going to... What? Threaten them and failing that—what?"

"You've a better plan?"

"Any plan would be a better plan, Barry. Just a plan. Any plan, at all. Think about what you're doing. You're job isn't to sabotage the other team. You're job isn't even to beat the other team. You're job is to make Nevers think that you have. You don't have to produce a ghost. You just have to make him think that you have."

"Right. You're right," I say and I nod. "What are you saying?"

"What they're doing doesn't matter. What you do matters. You need to learn about the girl and you don't need a graveyard or a magic shop to do that. You need a library."

"A library?"

"A library."

"Yeah," I say. "A library. I can find out about her in the library." Raising my head, I look across the street to find we are standing before the long front lawn of the Rockland Public Library.

16

The vaulted ceilings of the Rockland Public Library haven't changed much since I was a kid. They just seem a little smaller now, less imposing.

Just before me, a round circulation desk is staffed by a librarian who gives me a quick smile-and-blink. Turning arbitrarily from her attention, I step through a fancy wrought gate, coming out into a wide room furnished with overstuffed chairs—immediately turning again when I see that I've made my way into some sort of meeting. All of the chairs are full and a subdued, energetic conversation's passing around. Coming to a full stop, facing a display rack of magazines I stand, ineptly for a moment.

"What are you doing?" Ray asks.

"I don't know. I feel uncomfortable."

"It's a public building, Barry. You're allowed to be here."

I nod. I suppose he's right, but for some reason I still can't seem to make myself turn away from the magazines. Continuing to blink over the titles before me (Contemporary Sod-Home Design, Deuce: The Journal for Modern Twins, etc.) I say, "How do I do this?"

"You've been in a library before, Barry. You've been in this library before."

"In middle school. Should I ask about microfiche?"

"I'm not sure that's a thing, anymore." Ray's quiet a moment, thoughtful. "Computers," he says. "That's how people find things out nowadays. Computers."

"Computers." I nod to him and pull myself away from the magazine rack.

There's a couple free computers in the reference room and I take one realizing, after I have, that I don't know how to use it. Drives are key, I remember from my DOS days in the computer lab in high school. It's all about drives, I think, and I go through the list that I remember, which for some reason only consists of C: and D:.

The computer before me doesn't seem to care about drives, though. It's asking for a password. Hanging from the low privacy wall behind the monitor, a photocopied sheet informs me that guest passes can be arranged for at the front desk. I start to rise, when the occupant of the computer at my side says, "It's one-one-one, kin."

I turn, my mouth hanging open dumbly.

"The password, Cookie, is one-one-one. I don't even know why they bother with a password if their gonna use one like that." I sit back down and Drew smiles at me. "Seein' a lot of each other these days," he says as I key in the passcode. "Watcha looking up?"

"None of your fucking business," I say. "Private shit." The screen changes, displaying a view of the library from the front lawn and suspended over it, in the unremarkable foreground, are a bunch of file-tags. I blink at the screen. None of the files are C: or D:. And, at any rate, I don't have a floppy disk to feed it which, I now remember, is also necessary.

Continuing to watch as I sit and push the mouse around so it alights on different, meaningless options, Drew says "You don't know how it works, do you?"

"Of course I do. I'm not some sort of fucking..." I say, pushing the cursor around more aggressively. "Caveman! Maybe it would be easier if someone weren't staring over my goddamned shoulder."

Drew shrugs and turns back to face his own screen and, in a few moments, has gone to slouching, with his head planted in his hand, scrolling down a long page of photos. I keep at it with the mouse, selecting files and opening them and not finding the internet, which (I'm pretty sure) is where I wanna be. Which drive is it, though? After a few more moments, I say, "Okay, gimme a hint here."

Pushing his chair out, he leans past me to point down at the lower corner of the screen. "Okay, Caveman—right here, click this. That's the shortcut to Explorer." I click and the screen changes to a white screen with a blank text-bar. "Whatever you want, type it in that box there and you'll get some options to choose from."

"Yeah, yeah. I get it. It's just different from the ones I normally..."

"So you're all set?"

"Yeah, I'm all set," I tell him. He scoots back to watching his own screen.

Typing Josephine Nevers into the search bar, I press enter. After a moment the screen changes again—a number of articles line up that I quickly skim through. My hopes rise at the first in the list: Obituary for Josephine Nevers. I'm disappointed, however, when I look beyond the headline to the description and find that the article is about a death that took place in Kansas. In the late eighteen hundreds. Not the Josephine I'm after. As I continue reading down the list, only one item looks promising. The heading reads: J Nevers Antiques, Belfast, Maine and is dated from two years ago. Below the title is an excerpt: *I spoke with the proprietor regarding summer traffic and...*

Clicking on the heading causes the computer to go into a protracted spell of blank mulling and when it's finally done I'm left with the discouraging message: *Sorry, the page you are looking for on this blog does not exist.*

"How can it not fucking exist?" I hear myself say, perhaps too loudly. A pair of eyes surface over the privacy screen to give me a foul look.

Drew turns back to me. "What's the problem, Caveman?"

"Don't call me Caveman. This goddamned thing told me that there was this fucking article and I click on it and there's no fucking article."

"Okay. Okay. Calm down. Hit that back arrow, get back to the search engine." I do as he's asked and once I'm back to where I started he says, "So what are you trying to find?"

"This girl that went missing... I don't know... A long time ago. Josephine Nevers."

"Oh, shit kin," he says. "I know her mom. Lives off Pulpit Harbor Road on North Haven. Giant house, big iron gates out front..."

"You know her..."

"Her mom, yeah."

"That's great. That's fucking great," I say and I'm, again, maybe too loud. The guy across the privacy screen eyes me a second time and, returning his shitty look I spot, just behind him, stepping around the corner—Sarah Goldstein. Launching to my feet—raising a finger at her—I shout, "You!"

Her eyes flash on me before she turns away, to Drew at my side, saying, "Honey, we're going."

Standing and pulling on his jacket, throwing a backpack strap over his shoulder, he passes behind me, patting me on the back and saying, "Sorry, kin. Gotta scoot." They start away together toward the rear of the library.

Abandoning my computer to follow them, I announce, "Nice move the other day, getting me fucking robbed." I manage to keep my voice in a library-appropriate range, although the f-word does come out a little sharp.

Taking a moment to hiss over her shoulder at me, Sarah says, "Stay away from my son, Cookie." Turning her attention back to the boy, she warns, "And I know I've already asked you to stay away from him—I told you that, Drew."

"He sat next to me," Drew counters as they arrive at a second, bigger circulation desk at the rear of the library. This part of the building is newer—the ceiling tall and angular and dominated by rows of skylights. Digging around in her purse, Sarah and the librarian exchange quiet niceties while I loom, fuming behind them.

"You're just gonna fucking ignore me?"

After handing her library card across, Sarah gives me a sharp look. "I don't owe you anything, Barry. Not a thing."

"Owe me a couple hundred bucks, anyways. How much of that did Canth give you?"

She turns to me, full on. "Barry, this is a library."

"I know it's a library, damn it. We're surrounded by books and by... Fucking librarians... How much? I'll take that back, at least." My library tone is getting away from me. "Whatever Canth gave you, I'll take that."

"What's he talking about, Mom?" Drew asks and is ignored.

Frustratingly, Sarah's tone compensates for mine—every decibel I go up, she manages to drop one and, in the end, she sounds like the one who's in control. "Nothing. I got nothing from her. It was still worth it."

"I want my money," I say. I'm speaking loudly enough so that it acts as something of a cattle call—people are starting to look, to rise, to come and gather around.

"I want my money," she says.

"What the fuck are you talking about? We're talking about my money."

"I'm talking about my money. Drew's money. You think it's easy raising a boy..."

"Mom..."

"...On what Canth pays?" Looking at me, her eyebrows are arched up high, like a hawk fixed on prey. I blink back at her. "You're a piece of shit, Barry. You know that? A piece of shit."

The librarian is starting to look concerned as Sarah has given up on the transaction; given up on decorum, fully engaged with me now.

"I think this is pretty open and shut here," I say. "I mean, come on. You fucked me."

"Sir," the librarian beyond the countertop warns.

"I'm having a conversation, lady," I tell her.

"This is a library."

"I know it's a goddamned library. I wish people would stop fucking telling me it's a goddamned library." My voice is a full-on shout, now. "Look at all these fucking books! Look at your goddamned sweater! Your eyeglasses are on a fucking lanyard, for Christ's sake! Of course we're in a goddamned library! Look at these sad motherfuckers seated everywhere!"

The librarian continues on, "…Not a place for conversation. Certainly not a place for vulgarity."

"The first amendment…" I start in, but the librarian isn't having any of it.

"This is not a constitutional issue, sir. You cannot shout in the library."

"Yeah, Barry," Sarah gets in on it, too. "You can't shout in the library."

"Miss, I think I have this under control," the librarian takes an aside to scold her and so I smile. The librarian's frown only deepens and it's me she's aimed it at when she says, "You're going to have to leave, or I will have to call the police."

"What the fuck did I do to you, Sarah? I thought we were friends."

Drew warns softly, "Mom…"

"Why would you think we're friends? Why would you think that, Barry?"

Off guard, my voice shrinks in on itself, "We had, I don't know…"

"We had—what," she says. "A hookup in high school? What else did we have, Barry?" She gives me a break, a moment where I can think of nothing-much to say. "Anything? Anything, Barry? No?"

"I can't think of anything to say," I tell her.

"You can't think of anything to say? Nothing? How about 'I'm sorry?' That might be a starting point. You could tell me you're sorry. You could tell…" she starts, but when Drew says 'Mom' again, insistently from behind, she stops. She looks at me, waiting. "You're a child, Barry. You never did grow up. Probably better you ditched. Goodbye."

She turns to complete her transaction with the librarian, effectively shutting me out. There's some sort of momentum I can't account for and it's making my mouth keep moving, even after I wanna shut up, even after I've lost meaningful things to say and I'm blathering, "I've never even... And here you're saying something that doesn't even make fucking sense. I don't even know why you'd try to make me feel bad when you stole my fucking money..."

Drew keeps looking at me, just watching me with blank, wide eyes. From behind me some asshole's saying, "Listen, buddy. Why don't you just..."

My fists close up and I lower a shoulder, ready to turn, ready to spin around and lash out when Drew steps forward, throwing his arm over that low shoulder and turning me out toward the doors, insisting in my ear, "Come on, Caveman. Let's go outside. Get some fresh salt air. It's good for the spirits..."

17

~

Suddenly awake, I stare, panicked, into the darkness around me—uncertain for a moment about where I am. It's too warm for home. Too dark for prison, I manage to reason to some relief. Slowly, it comes to me. I'm on Meredith's couch again... or, still.

But, there's something—some intangible something—bothering me and I sit up, trying to pinpoint it. A dream?—if so, it's faded and gone already. A noise? I vaguely recall Ray's voice but now all there is to hear is the sump pump gurgling in the basement. It slurps and coughs and goes silent. Kicking the sleeping bag down to my knees, I writhe free.

At the end of the hall, the door to Meredith's bedroom is closed. Standing a moment to listen and hearing nothing but her soft snoring, I turn back around.

In the open gap of the front door, I whisper out into the night, "Ray?"

There's only the wind in the trees, hissing and clattering through the branches. Moonlight sits in stale puddles across the lawn. I try again, "Ray?" When nothing happens, I close the door to pull on my boots and jacket.

Chickawaulkie Pond is deep black—a black hole, a vacuum of light that I'm wary of. I stick to the far-side of the road. Walking down Route Seventeen I call out for Ray again and again, louder now that I'm away from Meredith's house; away from the worry of waking her. Still, no matter how I yell all I get back is the tired breath of the wind. The night's cold in my lungs, cold on the bare patch of skin on my wrists that won't fit into my pockets. Beyond the cold, a muted, barren worry nags me.

I don't realize, until I'm a hundred paces in, that I've turned off Route Seventeen and onto a narrow side street that climbs a hill. Passing an old shed with a crippled corner, the dull headlamps of a ride-on mower watch me from within. I pass a trailer home, the front lawn cluttered with welded tangles of sea serpents, tentacles arching and falling, twisted together in the moonlight. That I've never noticed this place seems absurd and makes me wonder if this is a dream that I'm passing through.

I pause a moment at reaching the eastern entrance of the Achorn Cemetery, before turning in.

The graveyard seems nearly day-lit, moonlight glimmering off the old limestone markers in the distant quarters. Something about the perfect, groaning peace of the wind begs not to be disturbed—maybe that's why I leave the paved pathway between the rows and start sneaking through the headstones. Creeping toward the obelisks clustered around the main entrance, I start thinking there's something more than that, though, keeping me quiet. There's something out there, drawing me in.

In the distance a dome glimmers and it's only when I'm closer that I realize it's a car and not the giant, rounded head of the sea-monster I'd first suspected. There's something familiar about the shape of it, though. Once I'm close enough I can tell why: it's a Prius. The passenger headlight is missing.

Too dark to tell for sure, but the car seems empty so I start moving again. Stepping out into the roadway I come up on the car. It is empty.

Here, on the rise where the car's parked, I can see out over the breadth of the cemetery. In the distant-darkness, near the tree where Ray and I met days before, a thin, twittery light plays between the rows.

Starting out after it, I stop after just two paces when something creaks behind me. Turning back, I just catch sight of the car jittering. I stand still, breathless, staring and waiting for it to happen again and almost falling over myself when it does. Again, it only goes on for a second, the car rocking slightly, the shocks squeaking before falling quiet and still.

Hooding my eyes with my hand to keep the moonlight off the glass, I check the windows again. For the third time, the car is empty. Couldn't be emptier.

The driver's door is unlocked. With the alarm blinging and the cab suddenly lit, I hurry to find the release for the hatchback, pry it up and step away, pressing my body against the door to close it quietly. With my eyes shut, I count to three, letting my sight readjust to the darkness before looking back out into the night. The light out there is frozen in place. Then, as though spurred by a starter's gun, it jolts into action and I catch sight of another, second light in the distance, also moving now.

"Fuck."

Hurrying around the car, I throw up the hatchback, a fresh burst of light spilling out across my face, across the dullness of nighttime. There, in the narrow trunk, an old steamer chest waits. The car shakes again—the steamer trunk jostling and I'm hesitant, a moment, about going nearer it. It could be anything in there—some nameless curse. The chupacabra. A porcupine, even.

Turning again, out into the graveyard—my night vision is completely dull now and I can only assume that I have very little time left. I go for the latch on the box. The mechanism click-clacks, the lid gasping open an inch. A glimmering blue light purls into the air from the thin gap.

Behind me, out in the cemetery, two voices have emerged from the night, calling faintly back and forth, getting louder. After a big, encouraging breath, I reach down and flip the lid all the way open, my eyes burned blind a moment by a brilliant enigma of staticky, blue light swirling in the walls of the box. Then, I recognize the shape of a man's back as it bulges out of the tight confines and a mess of tangly, glimmering hair as a head pulls free and I can hear him wailing distantly as he works to turn and face me. And then I see. It's Ray; his mouth curled up in horror, his skin glimmering with blue, electric ooze—his eyes gazing out black and blind.

It takes a moment before I find the nerve to reach in and grab him and drag him free. Dripping off as I pull him out, the ooze globs onto the ground, fading dim and cold there.

"Jesus, Ray," I say, getting my shoulder under him. Out, across the graveyard, the lights are closing in. The voices are recognizable now—Tomothy and Priscilla. I ask Ray, "You okay to move?"

He only groans, leaning up against me.

"We gotta move," I tell him and I drag him out, toward the main entrance on the Old Country Road.

I'm stumbling along as fast as I can, afraid to look over my shoulder, for fear of tripping, of falling, of making a mistake.

Coming out near the road I pull him into the backyard of an old farmhouse and scurry to a shed in a darkened corner at the back of the lot, sitting him down by the door and taking a moment to look back and catch my breath. I'm cold with sweat. Ray's left something of a glimmering trail to us that, as I watch, fades and starts to disappear.

Finding the shed unlocked, I help Ray inside, following him into the darkness and pushing the door almost closed behind us—almost closed, but leaving a gap to look through.

The Witch and her minion are out there, calling quietly, feverishly back and forth before a beam of light pokes around the hedges at the cemetery entrance and I hold my breath and watch Tomothy step forward, pausing to survey the ground with the beam of his lamp.

Behind him, unseen, Priscilla whispers, "They can't have gotten far; not in his condition."

Turning back to look at Ray, the glimmering ooze is already starting to fade, but he's shaking, his gaze aimed down at the soft, rotting floor. When I look back out into the night, Tomothy is gone.

18

"Okay. So, what was in the box?" Meredith asks. Blowing on her tea, the ghost of steam rising from her cup shudders and turns, leaning away from her breath. It's a bright day outside. The sun's shrill on the window ledge. It burns a patch of light on the living room floor. "*Was* it a porcupine?"

"It wasn't a fucking porcupine," I huff.

"Okay," she says as though I'm testing her patience. "Because you said, you thought it could be a goblin or a porcupine and the porcupine just seems like—you know—the more obvious of the two. 'Cause they're real. Unlike goblins."

"I wish I hadn't brought this up..."

She shrugs, takes a sip from her cup. "If you didn't want to talk about it—you're right; you shouldn't have brought it up. But you did. So, what was in the box?"

"I didn't, you know, bring this up so you could, you know, have fun at my fucking expense, Meredith. It's fucking serious and you're asking me about goddamned goblins..."

"You're the one who brought goblins into the conversation, I didn't..."

"Forget the goddamned goblins, damn it! Forget 'em! I'm just saying: there's like myriad fucking things that could be hiding in that goddamned box, you know? That was my only fucking point. Could be a beaver. Could be a seagull. There could have been the complete set of Longfellow's jerk-off journals in there, for all I know—it could be anything, is my point. It could be anything. That's all I'm saying."

Shrugging, she has another sip of tea. "The Longfellow thing wouldn't make sense, though." I frown. "Inanimate objects can't make a car move." Laughing at the sour expression she's managed to work my face into, she says, "So, are you gonna tell me or what?"

"It was Ray. Okay? Ray was in the goddamned box. That's what it was."

She inspects me—eyes peering out from the blind between her teacup and her lowered brow. Her lips purse together so tightly they go pale a moment. After another sip she says, "So... We ready?"

"That's it? That's all you're gonna fucking say? An hour and a half of busting my balls over it and that's all you have to say?"

"It wasn't an hour and a half. It was, like, five minutes, but you're right—it's a fucked-up dream. What more to say about it? You ready to go, or what?"

"Have you not been listening to me?" I ask. "It wasn't a dream, is what I'm telling you. I never told you it was a dream, anyhow. I'm telling you what I did last night, okay? I went to the Achorn Cemetery..."

"Barry," she says softly—in her tone there's a wash of concern. "You're trying to tell me, last night you woke up with a strange feeling that Ray was calling for you..."

"Not calling..."

"Whatever. You go outside, yelling for him. Managing not to wake me up..."

"I told you, I started yelling after I was out on the road..."

"...You walk all the way to the cemetery. There, you find a Prius with a broken headlight, which..."

"That's not important, the broken headlight thing." I shake my head, my face coloring. I'm still having anxiety over the bystander who spotted me in the alley. I hurry to say, "Let's just not even mention the Prius again, because, really, it's just not important..."

"Okay. Whatever. The car's jiggling. You open the trunk and there's a box in there. You think to yourself, there's probably some hobgoblin..."

"I was simply trying to illustrate the potential, varied holdings the box could contain..."

"You open it and—like a genie out of a bottle—poof! there's Ray, all corporeal and full grown. Is that it? 'Cause that's crazy, Barry."

I look away, shaking my head. "How is that crazy when twenty-five years ago..." I let the thought die. I've already said more than I want to and I clam up, looking away.

She's staring at me. I can feel it, even as I refuse to return her look. After a few, slow breaths, she says, "Twenty-five years. Can you believe that it's been twenty-five years?"

I keep looking away. I don't say anything. I just keep looking away, to the patch of light on the floor.

Through the silence between us, her breath marks out time. The quiet lasts so long that, when she speaks up again, her voice seems too loud for the room. "We've never talked about it, you know that?" I stand up and snag her cup from the coffee table, ignoring her when she says, "I wasn't done with that..." I bring it around to the kitchen sink, dumping the tea out and staring into the stain it draws as it rolls toward the drain. From behind me, she pipes up, "Twenty-five years and we've never once talked about it. That's strange, isn't it?"

I go to the cupboard and open the door and push the boxes inside around. "I'm hungry."

"Have you ever talked to anyone about that night, Barry? Other than the Coast Guard?"

I find a box of crackers and pull it down.

She's still talking, as I wrestle the plastic bag open and start stuffing crackers into my mouth. There's a certain edge in her voice. "Maybe it isn't just about you, Barry. You ever think about that? Twenty-five years and I don't even know. I loved him, Barry. He was my best friend."

I keep chewing, staring hard out the window and pushing crackers into my mouth.

"Sometimes it feels like he's still lost. I don't know even the barest details of his being found. And it feels like he never was. You loved him, too, I know that," she says. "But, he isn't just yours. He was mine, too. And your father's. He was everyone's and we all miss him. But you... You keep the whole thing, all the pain, like it only belongs to you." Cracker dust falls down my chin, littering my shirt and I brush it away irritably and stuff another handful of crackers into my mouth, even though my tongue already feels blistered by the salt. "Claire Andrews and her dad, you act like it isn't anything, your saving them. You pretend like it didn't happen. Does he still send you letters? You saved their lives, Barry. He reaches out to you and you turn away, like you blame him for what happened. It wasn't his fault; it wasn't anyone's fault. It was just something that happened..."

Meredith's still talking. She won't shut up.

"You live like you never did anything good. Like none of that ever happened. You work so hard to make everyone hate you; so afraid that you aren't the hero they wanted you to be. So, you make yourself a villain. But, you aren't. Not at the heart of it, you aren't. You're just scared..."

"Goddamn it!" I yell, spiking the box of crackers to the kitchen floor. The box crumples with a dry, rattling thump, crackers scattering out across the laminate. I kick the box and it hits the cupboard with another rattly thump, more crackers splashing up into the air, running across the floor. Finally Meredith shuts up. Only for a moment.

"What the fuck, Barry?"

"Goddamn it. Are we ready to go, or what?"

"No! Now you have to clean up your mess!"

19

Once Rockland's receded off the horizon, the ferry ride starts feeling like being lost at sea. But then, nearing the end of the hour trip, small islands start passing into view. The first are tiny, craggy black stones—blemishes on the otherwise uniform gray-green, inhospitable sea. A wind-tortured tree, clinging desperately to a parcel of stone, passes by. From here on in the islands become bulkier; colonized by ascetic looking trees and sickly grass, and the engine below us bellows, rumbling as the ferry slows and we enter into the channel between the islands of North Haven and Vinalhaven. Houses perched on hilly knolls blankly observe our arrival.

"So, explain how this goes—we knock on the door and…"

I shrug.

"No plan at all?" Meredith says, nodding silently. "That's a great starting point." Rapping her knuckles on the car's dashboard and pausing to pretend an imaginary door has opened, she says, "Ms. Nevers, we're here to ask some questions about your daughter. Why do we want to know about your deceased daughter? Just curious, that's all."

I sit on this a moment. "We could tell her the truth."

Meredith balks, barks out a solitary "Ha," and takes time to go through the whole dashboard-as-door routine again, before saying, "Ms. Nevers, how nice to meet you. We've been hired by your ex-husband to find your deceased daughter's ghost. He's concerned that she's haunting him from beyond the grave and is hoping for an exorcism. Perhaps you'd care to help. Won't you invite us in?"

"See," I say, "that sounds more reasonable."

The ship's hands scurry around the boat as it settles up against the pylons at the shoreside. Lashing the ferry up with huge tubes of rope, they finally open the chains at the bow and start directing cars off, through the low parking lot at the ocean gateway. The only restaurant in town is boarded over when we drive past. All the grandest homes seem abandoned for the winter as well.

As we head into the island's interior the houses shrink. The lawns stop looking so manicured. Evidence of a working life becomes apparent: a truck on blocks, a property walled off by stacks of lobster traps.

We run the whole length of Pulpit Harbor Road three times before determining, absolutely, that it hosts only one driveway barred by monstrous wrought iron gates. The house is hidden from view, behind a tangle of evergreens.

"Are you sure this is it?"

I shrug.

Staring at the gate, Meredith mutters, "This lady's never going to talk to us, Barry. Never-ever, in a million years."

"A little faith?" I ask and snap the door open and squeeze out into the cold day, crossing to a small speaker-box mounted on a post. There's no answer when I try the button; the speaker crackles emphysemicly, but that's all it has to say for itself.

"Told ya," Meredith says when I climb back in beside her.

"Go up the road a bit." I direct her to park off a dirt road that seems abandoned—tall, dun grass growing waist high, bobbing with the wind in the tract between the ruts. "You got gloves?" They're knit and she's already pulling them on.

Starting back up the road, toward the gate—before we've halved the distance—she yells for me to stop. Turning I find her stalled out, a half-dozen paces behind me. She looks small and lost in the empty road. "What's the plan? I mean, what are we doing, Barry? No one's there. No one answered the buzzer. That kinda of kills our plan doesn't it? No one to ask questions; no one to answer questions. Right?"

Under his breath, Ray is saying, "This is a bad idea, little brother."

"Don't worry about it," I say.

"We're not breaking in, if that's what you're thinking," Meredith says. "In case you don't remember, antics like that are the reason you need money so badly in the first place…"

"…Such a bad idea, Barry. Remember what happened last time—I told you that house wasn't empty and I…"

Turning from one to the other, so they both understand my seriousness, I announce boldly, "You can wait in the car if you want!"

Meredith looks confused and goes silent. Ray isn't so easily stifled—still talking, as though I haven't said anything at all, "You're gonna get your dumb-ass arrested, Barry. You're gonna get her dumb-ass arrested too… And there'll be no one to bail either of you out. Not to mention the fact that if you're looking for Josephine you're looking in completely the wrong place…"

"No one's getting arrested. I'm good at this," I say.

"No you're not." Ray laughs forcefully. "You suck at this, remember?"

"I do not suck at this," I say. "I am a good thief."

"I'm going to stop at this, 'cause I don't want to hurt your feelings," Ray tells me, "But, I just want you to know: you are a terrible thief. Maybe the worst ever and I'm not saying it to hurt your pride. I just think you need to have a more realistic self-image. I think it'd save you a lot of trouble. Probably save a lot of people some trouble."

"I'm a good thief," I insist one final time.

Ray shrugs. Meredith stands silent, frowning. Running through the trees, making them sway up in the narrow heights, the wind digs through the weave of my clothes. It's too cold standing like this. Turning her frown away, but keeping her eyes on me, Meredith asks, "Are you okay?'

"I'm fine."

Neither of us moves. She says, "I'm concerned, Barry. I was hoping that my tagging along would keep you from making bad decisions. But it seems you're determined to do stupid crap, regardless."

"She's right," Ray says.

"I thought you were done talking," I say.

Meredith's eyes go wide. "I've only just started talking. You know what, Barry? I oughta just take my car and go back by myself and… screw you! I don't need this garbage in my life. I'm an adult woman with an adult job and… I give up," she says and turns, starting back toward her car.

"Meredith," I say. "Stop." She keeps walking. "Please, just hear me out," I say and, finally, she stops—her back rigid. She won't turn, so I tell the back of her head, "I understand if you don't want to come inside. I get that. I understand if you wanna get in the car and just leave. I get that. But, you have to understand: I'm going into that house, whether you like it or not. I have to…"

Ray's saying, "Leave her out of this, Barry. Let her go back to the car..." maybe because he knows what I'm gonna say, before I've quite figured it out.

I keep going in spite of him, "And here's the rub, Meredith. If I go in there and you don't call the police, you're an accessory. You're breaking the law as well. So, you may as well come in with me, because that's where I'm going and we both know you aren't gonna call the cops..."

Meredith, during my oration, has turned, her eyes hard and cold, her face about the color of an eggplant. "You're an asshole, you know that," she says.

"So what if I am? It's bullshit anyways. You say I'm an asshole: you're an asshole, too. You go on about helping me, but that's not what you're after. We both know it. You know it. I know it. You're bored shitless, Meredith. It's painful to fucking watch. You sit in that quiet house, without cable—without so much as fucking cable, mind you—and you go to work and you come home and do nothing. You have this goddamned attitude like I've wasted my life —well, look at yours!

"So, go on. Sit in the car. Call the cops. Go home, read a book, take a nap—you might as well kill whatever time you have left on earth doing fuck-all-nothing. Either that, or you can come have a crazy-ass adventure with your crazy-ass friend, Barry, 'cause we both know that's the only reason you're here in the first god-damned place."

She blinks, looks at me. "That's not fair."

Ray's saying, "...Do you know how much effort I put into keeping this girl out of jail when she turned eighteen? Do not..."

I ignore him. "Fair or whatever—it's true. That's why you let me into your life, Meredith. Admit it. You're bored. You need some craziness, because you're fucking bored. You talk about what you wanted to do with your life since giving up acting and I find it super hard to believe that this life you've constructed is the substitute you've come up with—because you aren't doing anything at all."

"I'm an adult, Barry. This is what being an adult is…"

"Atrophy? What happened to the girl who liked the charge of being on stage? Where did the girl go who shoplifted for the hell of it? When was the last time you did anything fun, Meredith? Anything at all?"

She just looks at me, frowning. Her face has gone back to pale.

Ray's shaking his head. "I'm going back to the car," he says. "I give up. I give up on both of you."

20

Climbing to the top of the fence, I toss my leg over, throwing my body after it and trying to slide down the other side. I can't manage to hold on, though, so I fall, snapping branches and landing flat on my back. The ground, frozen hard, knocks the wind out of me. From beyond the fence, Meredith whispers, "Are you all right?"

"Yep," I wheeze and stand.

It takes her awhile to get to the top of the fence and once there she totters, looking down uncertainly. I tell her, "I did it; you can do it."

"You didn't do a very good job at it, though," she says, looking past me, intently to the ground at my feet. Shaking, she brings her foot over the spiked top rail, letting it dangle, struggling to get her other foot over. Pushing herself forward, she tumbles down, through the gap I broke in the branches, elbowing me in the face and landing on top of me. I hit the ground hard.

Brushing off her pants, she stands, saying, "You're right, that wasn't so bad."

I groan and sit up, holding my sore nose in my hand.

Keeping to the hedges alongside the driveway, we start away from the road. A few hundred feet in and around a bend, the driveway opens up to brick pavers laid out in an ornate courtyard. Finally the house is in view—french revival, I think: it's got a lot of fancy bullshit plastered all over it.

Grabbing my jacket, Meredith roughly pulls me back when I start out into the open. Shrugging off her grip I remind her, "No one answered the bell."

"That doesn't mean no one's here."

"It's usually a good indicator."

"...Could be in the shower... Could be listening to music..."

"There's no one here," I say. "There's not a single car parked out front." With a wink and a nod, I turn and strut into the open. Compensating for my bravado, Meredith crosses gripping my coattail, hunkered low, hiding behind me like I'm a walking hedge.

"...Sleeping... Doing Pilates... This feels wrong," she whispers, still hiding behind me and peeking out from around my elbow as we climb the wide, granite steps to the front door.

"Of course it does. We're breaking the law. It's supposed to feel wrong."

Reaching the landing, a wide, walnut door looks back at us. "...Watching a movie... Having sex... Shouldn't we knock?" Meredith whispers as I go for the knob.

"No. We should not. There's no one inside," I say. I shrug and say, "Plus—we were trespassing the moment we hopped the fence. There's no reason not to keep going."

"Trespassing?" Meredith hisses to herself. When I reach for the door handle, she begins chanting, "It's gonna be locked, it's gonna to be locked, it's gonna be..." cowering even lower behind me. I turn the knob. The catch thunks and the door yawns open. Turning to Meredith, I smile.

"...On a video conference... Doing aerobics..."

"No one's done aerobics since nineteen-ninety-five," I tell her.

"Why would it be unlocked if no one's here? If they're not planning on coming right back?" Meredith asks.

"I bet they never lock it; I bet the crime rate's obscenely low out here."

"Not right now, it isn't. Right now it's running, like, a hundred percent."

"You probably should have stayed in the car. Do you wanna go back?" She shakes her head no, but turns to look down the driveway longingly. "We tried the intercom. No one answered. There're no cars in the driveway. Right?"

Meredith nods. I push the door all the way open to step inside and she follows at my heels. The foyer is grand, but filthy—cobwebs hang from the chandelier overhead and rope the balusters on the staircase together. It's dark and ominous and, if it weren't for the homey warmth inside, I would suspect that the place had been abandoned for years. It's evident where some wall art has been removed; rectangular shadows lingering in the paint.

"Do you hear that?" Meredith asks.

"It's just the wind," I tell her without listening and start up the stairs.

"Where are we going?" she whispers, falling in line behind me.

"The bedrooms."

"How do you know they're up here?"

"Have you ever been in a house before? And stop whispering. There's no one here and you're making me nervous."

In spite of the size of the house, it doesn't take any searching to find Josephine's room. I lead Meredith right there, like I'd always known where it was, like I'd grown up going to that room. The walls are cluttered with posters hung at wonky angles—bands and movies popular a decade ago. The bed is made up in pink gingham.

"This must be her," Meredith says, hovering by a cork-board wall mat that's cluttered with clippings and photos. At Meredith's side, I spot the girl with no trouble. Her sharp, mischievous smile litters the collage.

"How do you know it's her?"

"She's in, like, all of the photos."

"Maybe she was a dyke; maybe that's the chick she was hot for."

"Maybe you're an idiot."

I shrug, mutter, "Maybe…"

My gaze drifts over the photos—people I don't know, places I haven't been. All that's obvious to me is what Meredith has already pointed out: Josephine is undoubtedly the girl: that blonde sprite peeking out from everywhere.

"Boyfriend," Meredith says, tapping a photo before moving away, to busy herself somewhere else. When she's stepped aside, I lean in to take her place. Checking out the picture, my fists curl closed. Though the photo must be ten years old, I instantly recognize Todd Rutter, sitting on a couch, his arm around Josephine. In a separate photo, on the same couch, they're kissing.

There are other boys, but not many—mostly it's Josephine and her girlfriends. Josephine with an arm slung over a friend's shoulders. Josephine and her clique pouting at the camera. Josephine and a friend sitting on her bed, playing with a store-bought seance board. That picture gets a tingle running along my scalp—like she's out there, waiting for me to reach her. Like she's been waiting a very long time.

Todd is in enough of the pictures so that his appearance is plainly meaningful, but when I step back, glancing over the greater montage of photographs, he becomes lost, just another face; as peripheral as anyone else sided by Josephine. And the photographs—I poke through them with my index finger—layers and layers deep of photographs, as though not one has ever been removed, only piled upon. Choosing one at random, glancing over my shoulder to check that Meredith isn't watching (I don't know why) I unpin a picture of Josephine. It looks like a year-book reject: she's sitting on a downed tree, leaning back, her smile's maybe a bit too sly for friends' parents to see. I tuck the picture away in my jacket and turn.

Pausing, with her head cocked and her eyes unfixed, Meredith says, "You don't hear that?"

We're both still, listening to a far-off whine, like a furnace charging. I say, "It's nothing."

Josephine's nightstand is packed with barrettes, small bottles of whatever-it-is-high-school-girls-keep-in-small-bottles, a big frilly lamp, a photo in a picture frame of Josephine with an elderly, milky eyed woman. Opening the drawer to the nightstand, I say "Lookie here." Catching Meredith's attention, I wag a flask of cinnamon schnapps at her.

"Gross," she says and turns away.

I take a swig and tuck it in my jacket alongside the photo.

"I thought we weren't stealing."

"Can you really call that stealing?"

"Yes. Absolutely. That's theft."

"It's finely aged, is what it is. Going to waste in the nightstand of a dead girl," I tell her. "Besides, she'd want us to have it."

From the same drawer that produced the schnapps, I find an envelope, ragged and brown and soft as cloth from years of handling. The page it holds is even more soft-worn.

"You know what's weird?" Meredith says. "The front entry looked like it was out of the Munsters, but up here, it's all clean and looked after."

"Wow" I say, the word escaping me without effort.

"What've you got?"

"Todd Rutter," I mutter.

"Who's that?" Meredith asks, not turning.

I nod to the wall mat. "The boyfriend. Kinda an enemy of mine too..."

"Enemy. You? Shocker."

"He's a poet," I say, casting the envelope aside to sit on the bed with the letter.

"Give me a line."

"This is a good one." I read, "*Like two ponds in moonlight, like twin moons in summer twilight, I'm lost and found, searching your milky orbs.* He must have struggled with a rhyme for orbs, it kinda fizzles out from there." I frown at the note and ask, "Milky Orbs? You think that's a fancy way of saying boobs?"

"I do not."

I hop off the bed. "I need to poop."

"I don't need to hear about it, Barry."

21

In the bathroom at the end of the hall I wash my hands, dry them; mesmerized a moment, gazing out the window to the back gardens and the sprawling ocean beyond. Wandering down, when my sight lands on the roof of a van, pulled up at a conspicuous angle near the foot of the house, my face goes hot. Now, that sound, that whirring, that Meredith kept bringing up—here in the bathroom it echoes metallically up through a vent in the floor: rising and drawing and fading and rising again in regular crescendo and now I know what that sound is. It's a vacuum, pushed and pulled and humming the whole time.

Trying to replicate how the bathroom was arranged before I came in, I quickly fix the hand towels. Was the door open or closed? I leave it open and quick-step back to Josephine's room.

"Look what I..."

I don't know if it's the finger to my lips or my ghost-pale expression, but Meredith goes silent immediately. Silent and still and it takes her a moment to lower the diary she's holding up as she mouths, "You son-of-a-bitch."

I just nod and start putting things back the way they were, closing up the nightstand and pushing the suitcase back under the bed where I found it. Meredith closes the closet and steps back and, after we've both examined the room quickly, she follows me to the door where I peer out, down the hall. The whine of the vacuum is clearer now, so evident that I wonder how I managed to ignore it for so long.

Tiptoeing, I lead Meredith to the stairs. The sound of the vacuum just gets louder and louder. Peering down into the foyer, I see our escape route is blocked. The woman vacuuming her way up the stairs flexes and uncurls her arm and hefts the vacuum, throwing it up on the next rise, climbing another step closer.

Scuttling back down the hall, we slip into Josephine's room. Why we've chosen this room is a mystery—the closet is stuffed full and even the space under the bed is filled with luggage. Stammering a moment, looking from corner to corner, finally meeting Meredith's gaze, I catch her mouthing, "I hate you."

I mouth back, "I know," and grab her wrist, tugging her back to the door. It's no good. The cleaning lady has cleared the top of the flight, now racing the vacuum down the narrow runner that tops the floor. Bringing Meredith back to the bed, I push her down and when she protests I give her a severe look and a harder push. Dropped down beside her, I force her under the bed and push my way in after.

"You idiot," she says. "We're sticking out."

I look and see—damn-it—she's right. Though we both fit— our fitting has pushed a suitcase out the far side. I start to move out, but it's too late, the maid's feet are already in the doorway, marching in.

The whirring is unbearable, watching with horror as the vacuum charges and retreats and charges again, growing closer with every thrust. Finally, no longer able to take the tension of watching it ascend on me in such lurching advances, I look away, turning to the dusty underside of the bed, where Meredith's lightening-white eyes peer from the dusk. Beating me in paced punches from shoulder to feet, the whirring of the vacuum and the hollow thump of it striking me effectively blocks out any trace of Meredith's vengeful giggling.

When the housekeeper finally arrives at the foot of the bed Meredith and I crane, in terrified unison, watching her feet as they fall past the corner. Nudging me, I wriggle out and turn to see Meredith wriggling as well, wriggling away and then turning and, just in time, pulling the escaped suitcase back beneath the bed. The vacuum and the maid wander away, doing rounds on the far side of the room. I can't see where she's gone and I stare at the ceiling, feeling naked. When Meredith goes into motion again I slither after her, back under the bed, just in time to see the maid's feet reappear.

Craned up tensely so my abdomen aches, I watch as the housekeeper's feet finally disappear out the door. In quick succession, Meredith punches me five or six times, whispering desperately, "You asshole. You giant, dumb asshole."

"We good."

"We are not good. We are screwed," she coughs quietly at me.

As the sound of the vacuum draws off, further down the hall, I squirm out from under the bed.

I'm happy to find, when I peek around the corner of the door, the housekeeper ducking into another room away from stairs. Meredith's just rising from the floor, brushing the dust from her pants. I whisper urgently, "Come on."

The vacuum noise growing ever more distant, Meredith and I rush quietly from the room, both of us looking backward, so intently watching over our shoulders for the cleaning woman that we're well in sight of the woman coming through the front door, by the time I realize she's even there. Luckily, she's fumbling with the latch as I catch sight of her, one of her arms cradling an overfull bag.

Grabbing Meredith's coat I yank her past the stairwell toward the open door at the far end of the hall. I'm moving so fast I almost pull her over and she stumbles to catch up with me. We make it out of sight as the woman at the door shouts, up the stairs, "Lilly?"

It must be the master bedroom where Meredith and I stumble. It's big; big wooden furniture tucked against the walls; big windows looking out on big views of bare trees, a big view of the cold ocean.

"Lilly?!" the woman, Ms. Nevers, I presume, shouts again.

I tug Meredith towards a closet door, but she fights against me and I turn to meet her rage-red face. "She'll change. She'll go to the closet and change."

I nod. We both turn to the bed. It's wider than the one in Josephine's room and we drop to the floor, scurrying beneath. Here, there's nothing beneath the bed—nothing but space and dust motes clinging along the wall. Space and dust bunnies and, now, two stowaways.

The whine of the vacuum cleaner finally dies and Meredith stares at me hatefully. "You get me arrested and I'm gonna cut your balls off."

"Relax," I whisper. "I've been in tighter spots than this."

"Have you?"

"I..." I'm not given space to finish because a pair of feet have appeared in the doorway, crossing the room, clapping right toward us. My breath catches in my throat when the bed squeaks and the feet flip away from sight.

The woman on the bed sighs, "Why do I still agree to do this?" For a moment it seems as though she's talking to herself.

"Relax, Joanne. Everything is taken care of." The feet of the housekeeper arrive at the door and stop there—I know it's her; those practical shoes will forever be imprinted in my brain.

"Everything? You're going to listen to Bill Waugh's inane droning all night?"

"He's just nervous. He has a crush on you."

"I'm too old for crushes, Lilly."

"Erica, Samantha, Andrew and I will be here at four with the caterer to get things organized."

"You're leaving me, then?" There is a great, flourished sigh.

"Don't be dramatic, Joanie."

Another sigh. "You're right. I know you are. Tell me what's left to do."

"Have a nice lunch. Have a drink, relax. Tonight will be fine."

"Fine?"

"Better than fine. Come, I'll make you a sandwich."

"And a martini?"

A laugh. "One."

There is a pause. "Thank you, Lilly. I really don't know what I'd do without you. I'll be down."

The cleaner's feet disappear and the bed creaks again, but the-ex-Mrs. Nevers doesn't get up for a moment or two longer. Her feet land beside my face and she crosses to the closet. Meredith jabs me in the ribs. Once Ms. Nevers has changed and left the room, after her feet pad down the hall until the sound of it spindles away to nothing, Meredith says, "I told you so."

I shrug.

"Well, this is beautiful," she says. "Did you catch all that? They're having a dinner party. We're screwed. The house is gonna be full of people and we're gonna be stuck and we're gonna miss the boat and I'm gonna miss work tomorrow and I'm gonna get fired. Thanks, Barry. Thanks."

"You got your cell phone," I say. "Call out."

"Now?"

"This might be the only chance you have."

"You're an asshole." Meredith does a decent job of making her whisper sound sick, as she explains to her boss, "No. No. I'm sure I won't be able to come in tomorrow... I'm sure." She's silent for a moment after hanging up. "Did I mention you're an asshole?"

The room gets dark. The house goes quiet. Joanne Nevers does not return to the bedroom; only the odd scrape of furniture being moved, the knock of cabinet doors closing lets us know that she's still here—only those sounds keep us beneath the bed. Meredith and I lay, side-by-side and mostly silent as the afternoon wanes to evening. Mostly silent, but for an occasional, whispered, "Asshole," from the darkness at my side.

22

Just past dusk, the quiet of the house is broken by the doorbell and a subsequent eruption of greetings from the front hall. The party fills in, in quick, stuttering stages, first announced by the doorbell and then the doorbell stops ringing and it's only boisterous hellos and cheers that mark the arrival of new guests. Music starts up: a pulsing drum beat rattling the floor behind my back. Soon it's loud enough that Meredith and I no longer feel bound to speechlessness.

"Asshole," she says.

"How many people do you think are down there?"

"The island. All of them. Every last one."

"It sounds like a lot, doesn't it?" I say.

"Don't get any ideas, Barry."

"I got an idea I don't want to spend the night under this bed."

"Better than a cell."

"I doubt this island even has a cop," I say. "If we don't make a move, we're gonna be here until the party leaves and Joanne comes up and gets into bed and sleeps a full night and gets up tomorrow and... Shit, what if she's planning on spending the day in, cleaning? Even worse—what if your snoring wakes her up?"

"I don't snore. And, I don't think women who keep houses like this do the cleaning themselves."

"Did you hear her moving the furniture around?"

Meredith's silence seems to agree. She says, after a moment, "Your plan…"

"Get out. Take a look. Feel out our options."

I can barely make out the silhouette of her face, her round brow, her nose. "So explore. Asshole. Let me know what you find."

"You're coming, 'cause if I find a way out, I'm taking it."

She grumbles. "Fine."

In the hall outside the bedroom there's nothing to be seen, nothing but an orange effervescence of light smudging the ceiling from the floor below. Looking down from the banistered precipice above the stairs, shadows bob across the opposite wall and the tops of a few heads, and the open, golden orbs of drinks in hand, can be seen. Through one of the sidelights flanking the front door, I catch sight of a handful more guests climbing the stairs to the house. Ducking back behind the wall, I take a nip from Josephine's schnapps.

"What'd you see?"

I shrug, stow the bottle back away in my coat. I say, "A gumshoe. A wizard. The Tin Man."

"A Halloween party? Explains the cobwebs in the foyer, I guess," she says with a sigh. "And here we are, dressed like a couple of schlubs." Looking me up and down, she corrects herself, "Well, one schlub at any rate."

"Nice, that your attitude has improved."

"An impromptu costume idea: We could tell people you're an idiot and that I'm your caretaker."

"We could tell people you're a know-it-all shrew."

"Doesn't sound like a costume," She says. "Here's one: you as a eunuch. We'd just need to do a little rearranging. Not much at all." She cracks her knuckles. After a moment, she says, "I think we can just go, don't you? I mean, we walk down the stairs, we get to the door—the place is packed with people, even with us not being dressed up, no one's going to notice, right?"

"Shit. I think you're right."

"I mean," Meredith says, working herself up, standing away from the wall. "Even if someone does stop us, it's like, whatever. We haven't been poking around here. We haven't been hiding under beds, stealing schnapps. We just saw the crowd and wandered in. Right?"

"Wandered in. Yeah," I say. "I think you're right. Let's go," and I'm full of optimism now. The two of us nod confidently back and forth to each other. After the round of confident nods, we stand idle. Meredith nods again. I gesture for her to pass, but she doesn't move.

"Why am I going first?"

"It doesn't make any difference which one of us goes first," I say.

"Right," she agrees.

"Right," I say and I gesture again for her to go.

"So—why am I going first?"

"It doesn't matter who goes first."

She frowns at me. "Yeah. I get that, I just don't know why it has to be me."

"It's your plan," I say.

"And you're the stupid jerk who got us stuck in this situation in the first place. Furthermore, you're the stupid-jerk-reason why I'm losing a vacation day tomorrow," she says, her voice rising.

"I thought you agreed that it didn't matter which one of us goes first."

"It doesn't matter," she insists, jabbing the air with her finger. "But it sure-as-heck isn't going to be me."

"Okay. Okay." I throw up my hands and turn, taking a deep breath and stepping into the puddle of creamy light beaming up from the foyer. No one down there turns. We don't so much as raise a look as we descend the stairs.

Thriller is on the stereo. The din of talk and music is raucous, but even then, I find myself stepping gingerly as we descend, as though my footsteps could be heard over the blaring music. Meredith nudges me in the back. "You look conspicuous. Loosen up."

"If you don't like the way I do shit, you should have taken the lead," I say. But, she's right and I shake out my arms and I force myself to smile and nod as we pass by a cowboy on our way to the front door. Once there, I turn, looking back over the party. The room is half dark; costumed party-goers half hidden in darkness. A mirror ball turns, spangling them and the walls as *Thriller* comes to it's conclusion, giving way to the *Monster Mash*. Meredith tugs my sleeve. She already has the door open, pulling me out into the night, even as the night air rushes in, weakly trying to hold me back.

As we trot down the front stairs, I'm having that feeling of a barely-free man—that feeling that, at any moment, this could all fall apart.

The driveway's lined with cars. Past the light of the courtyard, the parking becomes more haphazard: cars half-pulled into the hedges, a field obstructed with trees looks like a wrecking yard— cars cluttering the spaces between the trunks, beneath the branches.

It's dark out here and there really is no reason I should see it, but suddenly, seized up, I stop.

"What is it?" Meredith asks, staring into the darkness, too.

Uncoupling from her I step out into the field. It's a bright night, the moon and stars spangling the tops of the cars that I pass between. A row in, I stop, my hand resting on the hatchback of a Prius, parked beneath a walnut tree. It's a bright night, the moon and stars conspiring to show the bumper stickers cluttering the backend of the car: I Heart Miracles, Astral-Projectors Make Better Lovers, Reincarnation Saves Lives.

Behind me, Meredith mutters, "Headlight's broken…"

"I have to go back," I say.

Meredith blinks at me. "I don't think I heard that right. Say that again."

"I need to go back."

"You're going back? After we spent six hours hiding under a bed, waiting for an opportunity to escape—you're going back?" She tilts her head. "You realize how insane that is?"

"I'm sorry…" I say. I've already started my return to the house.

The facade is lit up with spotlights, etching deep shadows into the garlands above the windows. The sidelights by the front door flash in time to the thunder of music.

"Barry, don't you do this to me," she pleads. But I don't turn and I don't hear anything more from her.

23

By the time I come back through the door, the *Monster Mash* has been replaced by an insipid contemporary song with a booming beat and ear-blistering female trilling—but the rhythm sets the pace and I start into the throng on the dance floor, winding my way between the bodies, searching for the Witch.

Complicating the search are the costumes: both the muscled barbarian and the french maid with whom he's dancing can easily be ruled out, but the foam-rubber Potato-Head Man gyrating in the corner takes thirty seconds of hard staring before I rule him out as well. Even then it's only guesswork: Potato Man keeps grabbing his crotch `a la Michael Jackson, in spite of *Thriller* long ago having concluded. I cross the dance floor once and then again and then a third time, finally exiting the crowd into a lit hallway on the trail of an ogre who, once we've emerged into a bright kitchen, I quickly determine is not Priscilla.

Here, guests circle an island laid out with refreshments. Pulled into the queue, I help myself to a beer from an ice-bucket to wash down a sandwich that I end up not taking. Stepping away from the buffet, I survey the scene. A team of caterers works, restocking the food and drink as it's depleted. Meanwhile, the guests mostly don't linger. They snag snacks, fresh drinks and exit through the hallway, back toward the booming music.

At the front of the kitchen some partygoers have congregated around a long table, to play a drinking game, and beyond that crowd, in a room shuttered off with french doors, a smaller, more intimate party has gathered. I down my beer, insert myself into the line to quickly grab another, and make my way to that further room.

Inside the doors, another pair of caterers make rounds with trays of hors d'oeuvres and flutes of champagne. The air here is formal. The guests assembled aren't costumed, are older and quieter—for the most part quieter. The exception being a round, red faced man in the back who seems intent on being heard by everyone. "So, the deal was no good. I told Bartlett that from the start. He says to me, 'This kid's on his way up!'" The fat man shakes his head. "I said, 'If you think that kid's on his way up, Bartlett—I'm afraid you're on your way out!" The fat man laughs. "I swear I did, Joanne! I swear, that's what I said!"

Knocking back half my beer, I get out of the doorway and start toward the fat man and the bored looking lady enduring his anecdote. From seven yards away, when our eyes meet, the look she gives me cries for help. She just keeps staring at me as I close in, a warm, thankful smile spreading over her face, the closer I get.

Before I'm even to her, she's risen from her chair, extending her hand, allowing me her fingertips. "Joanne Nevers?" I ask.

"Yes! Mr…"

"Cook," I say.

"Mr. Cook! I've been so looking forward to meeting you," she says enthusiastically. Looking down to the fat man, who's face has fallen, she says. "I'm so sorry, Bill, you're going to have to excuse me, but I've been waiting all evening to finally get a chance to say my hellos to Mr. Cook."

The fat man grumbles while Joanne encourages me to lead her away. She's beaming as we cross the room. Patting my arm, she says, "Thank you, so very much for that. I've been cornered in that chair for the last hour and a half. I think I might have gone partially deaf in this ear."

"Happy to help," I say.

Arriving by a table, as far away from the fat man as the room will allow, she releases me, snatching a flute of champagne from a tray that's passing by. After a sip, she says, "Well, we've come all this way so that I can catch up with the eminent Mr. Cook, so I suppose I should at least ask what it is he does."

"Oh," I say. "I'm not big on talking about myself..."

"That's a change," she says and tilts her glass again, smiling at me as she sips. "But, please indulge me."

"I'm sort of an oddjobber, I guess—I have a bunch of different projects in the works right now. Some legal endeavors, maritime work, uh... Paranormal investigations. A pretty mixed bag..."

"That's quite a range. Have you met Priscilla Bloomfield? She's around here somewhere. Owns a shop in Rockland, I guess. I met her earlier this evening. She does fortune telling and things of the sort. You two might have a lot to talk about..."

"Perhaps. Honestly, there are a lot of questionable parties involved in my sort of business. Truth be told: she's the focus of one of the jobs I have going right now."

Joanne nods earnestly.

"Did you know that she's a huckster? A conman. Or, woman in her case. If you'd call that lumpy, spiky-haired thing a woman..."

Joanne's nodding has grown slower, her look a little concerned.

Nervous about the slowing of her gestures, I start talking more rapidly. "She tells people that she can communicate with the dead—actually, what she's doing is luring them into a trap. She has this box that she captures spirits in. I don't know the exact purpose of the box but, I've seen, first hand the victims of it and, let me tell you, you wouldn't want your beloved in there." A frown's crept up on Joanne's face. "I mean, imagine Jo…"

A caterer, holding up a tray of hors d'oeuvres, plants himself in front of us, interrupting me before the name Josephine is even out of my mouth, saying, "Mr. Cook. There's an urgent call for you." Turning to face the kid holding the tray, I find Drew staring back at me. "A very urgent call. Very urgent."

"A call?"

"Yes. An urgent call. A very urgent call."

Seizing the interruption, Ms. Nevers pats me on the arm and says, "Thank you again. It was very nice meeting you, Mr. Cook. I have other guests…"

Frantically, I try to get her to stay. She smiles and nods, ignoring me and pulling away. Drew's still fixing me with that look when he says, "This way, *sir*."

"What's this bullshit about a call?"

"This way, sir," he repeats coldly.

Leading me through the kitchen, he doesn't say anything more until we're back in the hall, heading toward the dance floor. "What the hell are you doing here, Cookie? You working the rounds?—seeing how many places you can get kicked out of in a week?"

"What the fuck are you doing here?" I volley.

"I'm working."

"Well, I'm working, too," I tell him.

"Really, 'cause it looks like you're crashing a party and trying to upset my employer." Escorting me to the end of the hallway, Drew holds his ground at the threshold. "Apparently, though, I'm the only one—so far—who knows you're crashing. So, do me a favor, Caveman, and stay in here. Out of the way. Don't make me blow a whistle on you."

I nod, grabbing a glass of champagne off his tray and leaving my empty beer bottle in its place. "Deal. But if you see Priscilla, that purple haired lady with the Prius, you gotta come and get me."

"You're trying to make deals with me?"

I shrug. "I'm sure I could work out a way to get us both removed, if you'd prefer that."

His eyes narrow. "Don't make a scene," he tells me before turning back up the hallway.

Moving away from the blaring speakers I saddle up alongside a lady in doctor's garb, near the back of the room. When she offers a smile I yell over the music, "I'm looking for a short, fat lady with purple hair."

"Priscilla, was it? I saw her a while ago. Or were you looking for that punk girl?" she asks, pointing to a girl adorned with a mohawk-bald-cap out on the dance floor.

"You know her?"

"The punk girl?" she says, shaking her head.

"Priscilla."

"I met her earlier. She's the first lady with purple hair I've met since nineteen-ninety-four. Kinda sticks with you." Looking me up and down, the doctor asks, "What are you supposed to be?"

Looking down at myself (work boots, jeans, a flannel shirt) I say, "Lumberjack?"

"You look kinda like a guy who just dressed in his regular clothes to come to a costume party. You know what I mean?"

"You see, you're wrong. My nine to five is, I'm actually a cat burglar. Normally I do traditional black when I'm on the clock," I say.

"The difference between a cat burglar and a regular burglar?— I've always wondered."

"Gracefulness, athleticism."

"...Hairballs?"

"What is it that you do?"

Bashfully smiling, she says, "I'm a nurse practitioner," and I laugh. "I hate getting dressed up for things like this. The scrubs, at least they're comfortable."

"Like pajamas, right?"

She nods. "Honestly, sometimes I just wear them around the house; sometimes to bed."

"Probably shouldn't tell patients that."

She nods. "Probably not."

"Downfall of scrubs?" I say. "Shallow pockets."

"No good for a cat burglar, that's for sure. Hey," she says, nodding toward a row of doors at the back of the room. "Isn't that her—back there?"

Everything in here is either black, mirror ball spangled or some murky in-between, but across the room I just catch sight of a figure ducking out through the doors. It's impossible to tell if it's her, but the shape seems about right: stocky, crazy hair. It's either her, or someone dressed up as a pineapple. I thank the nurse and excuse myself, starting toward the door.

Out onto a patio, away from the noise and the crush of bodies, the night is cold and empty. The house runs off in both directions and I can't make out anything in the shadows, but it's hard to believe Priscilla has gotten away so quickly; it only took me a few moments to get after her.

A stone walkway leading away from the house seems her only likely exit, and so I start down it, winding my way through the wide, moonlit gardens. Even as the path stretches away from me, half-lit, toward the ocean, I catch no sign of Priscilla. Still, I keep moving, the ocean bellowing louder and louder.

Where the lawn gives way to an arching, shale cliff, I come to a stop.

On the pebbly beach below are two figures—a pineapple, (Priscilla, I assume) with her back to me, and facing her… Even at this distance, there's no denying it's her—the ghost, Josephine.

For all the constant swimming of the pale veils enveloping her, Josephine stands still. Her face is ashen, radiant in the moonlight. Gesturing wildly in the face of Josephine's serenity, whatever incantation the Witch is pronouncing is lost to the wind and the clamor of the sea. Though I've managed to get my breath back, it takes a moment longer to get moving again. Priscilla is certainly a danger to Ray, but—as I reach the first step of the staircase leading down to the beach—I realize she must be a grave threat for Josephine as well. Whatever torture she'd subjected Ray to in that steamer trunk, there's no doubt the Witch wouldn't hesitate to practice it again on the fragile specter before me. I take the stairs two at a time. The thought of poor, radiant Josephine stuffed in a box and gagging on soupy TV static gets me running.

Landing on the beach, I call out, "Hey, Witch!"

The tone of my voice snaps Josephine out of her trance: picking up her veils she turns, retreating into the night.

"Mr. Cook, what are you doing?" Priscilla yells back at me.

"I got my brother back," I say, marching along. With pebbles slipping under my feet, I stumble, but keep going. "I'm not going to let you take that girl, just because you've come up with some new storage space in your evil fucking box."

"Mr. Cook, you do not know what you're talking about."

I'm almost to her and I haven't slowed a bit. I haven't slowed, but it's dawning on me that I don't know what I'll do when I get to her.

"Mr. Cook, if you come any closer," Priscilla warns, but she makes the threat too late, I'm almost on top of her—any closer and we'd be having intercourse. Her threat's too late to deter me but her hand swings out and I feel something collide with my ribcage just before the world goes fiery hot and tingly and I fall to the ground.

There's a horrid lingering-tingle of that hot-rodded-electrical-charge running through me as I blink and sit up. Priscilla is gone, but behind me I hear the clap of footsteps on the stairs. Wrestling up, I turn to see Priscilla disappear over the shale berm above. Weak legged, I start after her. The shock took a lot out of me. I'm wobbly coming back along the beach and have to use my arms on the stair rails to pull myself up into the backyard.

She's just a little ahead of me in the garden when I finally get there. Starlight glistens in her short, tufted hair, when she turns, fixing herself in place to challenge, "I'll do it again, if you don't leave me be."

I continue on, "Stay away from my brother. Stay away from the ghost, Josephine."

"You don't know what you're talking about, Mr. Cook," she says. Poised like a wall, she triggers a little blue spark at the end of her hand by way of a threat. Just the sight of that dancing blue bolt sends a jolt of panic through me and this time I manage to put the breaks on. Raising my hands, I stop. "Leave, Mr. Cook. Get going."

"You can't have my brother."

"You don't know what you're talking about, Mr. Cook. You're like a figure in a snow globe—you have no concept of the world beyond your immediacy. The machinations of the universe are at play, Mr. Cook; they do not care what you think or how you feel." The thump-thump of music from the party echoes off into the trees.

"That's a bunch of goddamned gibberish, Witch, and you know it. My brother is my brother. We're blood," I insist. "We belong to each other."

"Your brother belongs to Samsara. He is not yours to own."

"Fuck you," I say and without thinking, forgetting entirely the stun-gun in her hand, I start forward again. It doesn't take me long to remember. Before it even takes me to the ground, I remember. At it's staticky little cackle I remember but, it is, of course, too late by then.

24

The wind is hard and cold in the first dull light of day. Looking out over the channel to Vinalhaven, Ray has that look in his eyes again. That same look he had in the cemetery—gray, spinning, far off; hard-focused on something beyond my sight.

"Ray? Ray, you said something yesterday about Josephine not being here. Where is she? Can you see her?"

It's like he doesn't hear me, even after I've asked again. Waving my hand through the path of his vision, he just keeps staring out. It's too cold standing here, staring along with him so, when I don't get an answer, I come down off the rocks and cross the clearing to Meredith's car. The windows are fogged over, gray. Tugging her jacket up closer under her chin Meredith shifts in the driver's seat when I climb in.

"Where'd you go?"

"Had to pee," I say and she closes her eyes again and starts snoring instantly.

I take Josephine's diary down off the dashboard and start flipping through it.

It's hours before Meredith wakes, yawning, stretching, rubbing her eyes. "How long've you been up?"

I flip through some pages, skipping to the last one. "T won't stop calling me and mom's getting pissed."

Meredith shakes her head and rubs her eyes again and blinks, "Huh?"

"Here," I say. Flipping back through the book, I read aloud, "I just can't take T any longer. I went over to the Gramercy's house last night. Bethany was baby sitting and wanted company. I told T I was going there and—what's he do?—shows up, expecting to hang out. Bethany didn't say anything, but you could tell it was awkward for her..."

I look up from the text to Meredith. Blinking back at me she rubs her eyes again. After a moment she says, "It's a little early for this, Barry."

"Here," I say. "Check this out." I skip forward some pages. "Broke up with T today. Did not go well. When he walked away, he started attacking the picket fence on the Collins' front lawn, tore out a post and beat a tree with it until it broke in two. It was really scary. So happy Bethany was there. Not sure anyone would have believed me if I hadn't had an eyewitness. T is a total spaz." I look to Meredith again.

"I need coffee."

"Come on, Meredith. These are huge revelations, here."

"Right. T is a total spaz. It's very illuminating, Barry." She sits up, adjusts her seat back so that it flops up to meet her.

"Come on, Meredith... T as in Todd..."

"Or Trevor, Travis, Tomothy..."

"Did you just say Tomothy?"

She shakes her head. "Timothy. Why would I say Tomothy? That isn't even a name. My point is, though, Barry, T doesn't necessarily mean Todd. It could mean anything. Hell, it could be this mystery boy's last name, it could just be some random code that Josephine made up."

"Why the fuck would she do that?"

Meredith shrugs. "Heck, maybe it's not even her diary."

"What the fuck are you talking about?"

"We just don't know, Barry..."

"We found it in her room."

Again Meredith shrugs, a gesture I'm finding particularly obnoxious this morning. "She could have been holding it for a friend. She could have stolen it from someone. A sibling could have been storing it there for safekeeping."

I flip to the inside cover of the book and show Meredith the inscription, at the same time saying, and pointing to the line, "Here, written in pen—Property of Josephine Nevers."

"Okay," Meredith shrugs. "So, it's probably hers."

"Probably? This is her diary. Her room is littered with pictures of Todd. We found a poem that Todd wrote. T is for Todd and T killed her."

"Where does it say that?" she asks, leaning back.

"How would it say that? How does a victim of a homicide write in her own diary 'Oh, by the way, today Todd murdered me.'"

"T," Meredith corrects.

"Are you intentionally being obtuse?"

"I, Barry," she says, "am trying to balance out your lunacy so that you don't get tasered again. That sounds nice, doesn't it?—not getting tasered again."

"It wasn't a taser. It was like a stun gun," I say. "Listen, the last entry is about how Todd..."

"...T..."

"...Todd. Is stalking her. Come on, Meredith."

Looking away, she says, "Okay. So let's pretend we have enough evidence here to do... What? What are you proposing we do? You gonna tell Nevers his daughter was murdered, based on this? When the cops come knocking at your door what are you gonna tell them?"

"Let's go talk to Todd."

"Todd—your professed enemy—Todd?" She lets out a mirthless little laugh. "That would be great. I'm trying to keep you from getting tasered and you're trying to get yourself shot. No way, Barry."

"We have another hour and a half before the next ferry and after that we'll still have another ferry that we can make today. You've got the whole day off."

"Thank you for reminding me of that. Actually, watching you get shot might be a nice way to spend this unscheduled-vacation-time."

"He did it, Meredith. He killed her. That's the last entry, that one about him calling the house all the time. We need to go confront him."

"Let me see that," she says and I hand the diary off to her. "Look," she says, holding the book open for me. "It has to be the last entry, Barry. It's the last page in the diary. There's no room left…"

"Look closer."

Her eyes are barely open and she's shaking her head. "What am I looking for?"

"Along the binding there—pages have been ripped out…"

"So…"

"So maybe Todd knew about the diary. Maybe there was something more incriminating…"

"This is crazy…"

"I know," I say. "That's why we have to…"

"I think you're missing what it is I'm finding so insane about this, Barry. I think you're missing it entirely." Shaking her head, folding the book closed, she sets it back on the dashboard, beyond my reach. "Besides, we don't even know where he lives," she says.

"I do." This may not be entirely true: I do know where the house sits on the coast of the island. I've seen the house before; had it pointed out to me. Whatever road it's on, however…

"No way."

"I need to know," I tell her and I'm already going for the door handle, wrenching it open and stepping out into the blustery morning.

"Where are you going?"

I shut the door.

Ray's come down off the rocks to join me as I head out onto the empty road. I'm happy for the company and, as we head away from shore, that droning vacancy in his gaze seems to subside.

A ways up the road, Meredith rolls up beside us. "Get in," she says. I keep walking, aimed forward, raising my hand dismissively.

"It's cold out, Barry. Don't make me drive with the window down."

I keep walking.

"You're gonna get yourself killed," she says. Sighing violently, she quickly accelerates, cranks the wheel and slams the breaks so that the car lurches to a stop, blocking my path. "Get in," she tells me.

"I have to do this, Meredith."

"Get in. I'll go talk to him for you."

Bending down, into the window, I tell her, "You might think it's silly, but I'm pretty convinced that this is a murder we're dealing with."

"Yeah. Yeah. Get in," she says impatiently, no longer looking at me at all.

25

"You told me you knew where it was," Meredith says while retreating from a road clearly marked *Private*. "We're not missing the ferry again. You have ten minutes to find this place," she tells me and I agree, but suspect I've no real choice in the matter.

It takes a few more failed attempts before we finally find the house. Resting beyond an exposed plate of ledge just before the gray, windswept ocean, the house is small, rickety and worn, the gray wood clapboard mottled with paint chips. Out on the water, *The Bloody Rudder* heaves and falls among the waves, lashed to a mooring.

"You sure this is it?" Meredith asks. She's parked conspicuously far from the house.

"That's their boat."

"Okay," she says, starting out of the car.

I lay my hand on her wrist, gently stopping her. "If you're not back in ten minutes, I'm coming in after you."

Her look is no less sincere than mine when she tells me, "If you come in after me: I will make you a eunuch."

I nod because it seems like she means it. Stepping out into the wind, she crosses the lot to the front door. No truck in the driveway, no car; I'm surprised a moment later when the door to the house opens to swallow Meredith and closes again. I sit, waiting.

Gray and frothed with white, the water rolls and I look at the clock again and again, worried that it's broken—the minutes stretch out endlessly. The Rutters must be one of the few fishing families left out here with waterfront views and it makes me wonder why they stay. The property must be worth hundreds of thousands and yet, here they've perched themselves, cutting a meagre existence from what the ocean will offer.

"What do you think?" I ask Ray's eyes in the rearview. "Do you think Todd killed her?"

"I think you're losing sight of the plan again," he answers.

"If it was a murder…"

"I also think you shouldn't be getting Meredith involved in this, for the record."

"They've got that boat, right there…

"I also think you ought to give Pa a call. When did you last talk to him?"

"Her body could be anywhere…" I say. "What if it's buried here? Right on this very lot? That would make sense then, them not selling it…"

"You're right," Ray says. "Someone holding onto a property in the face of financial hardship… That's highly suspect…"

"Right?"

Shaking his head, frowning, he looks out the window. After a moment he says, "Did I ever tell you about Sharon Wickworth…"

It's only been five minutes, according to the clock, but Meredith's continued absence and the stillness of the house—the darkness lingering in the windows—bothers me. I only manage to make myself sit still for another minute (by the car's clock, which I suspect can't be trusted).

Letting myself out, into the wind, I'm aware now of how exposed I am. The property, save a few scrubby bushes bent by the wind, is bare and flat. I move like I'm heading to the front door but once I'm close enough, I duck off abruptly, pushing up against the house to hide beside a window.

Looking in at an angle, I find the back of a man's head. Slowly widening my view, I light on Meredith. There's a steaming cup of something in her hands. Bringing it to her mouth to blow and sip, her eyes flash on mine—her face suddenly pale and stiff. We only hold eye contact for a moment before she looks away, her face spasming back to a warm, slightly-alarmed smile. She nods to Todd and blows mechanically at the cup again.

Whatever it is he's saying, the words are lost, just the murmur of his voice emerges through the glass. For a few more passing moments Meredith doggedly continues to avoid looking at me. Moving so I'm standing centered in the window, I finally manage to catch her eye—but only briefly.

What was that look?—fear? There was something in her eyes, a desperate, impassioned sort of look. Unsure what it was meant to indicate, I'm hesitant about launching in to the rescue. No, I need to be sure, so I start waving my arms.

When she looks again, I quickly mouth, "Are you okay?"

Her face is hard; again, that impassioned look in her eyes. She gestures for me to get out of the window, so I rush to ask, silently, "Are you in danger?"

She isn't given time for a response, Todd has returned his attention to her. Setting her cup aside and standing, half bowing she looks like she's apologizing for something, a little red-faced as she steps away from the chair. When she crosses the room, headed to the door, I step out of the window, moving to meet her.

She's not wearing her jacket when she comes outside. Hugging herself, shivering against the wind, she looks at me. "What are you doing?"

"Are you in danger?"

"No, I'm not in danger, you idiot. Get back in the car."

"Are you sure? You seem agitated."

"I am agitated," she says and looks at me long. "Go back to the car, Barry."

"You're sure?"

The look she levels on me, I wouldn't know whether I'd describe it as hot or cold, but whichever, it is the extreme of that. "Listen to me," she says. "I am only doing this because you made me. I do not want to be doing this, do you understand?"

I nod.

"No," she says. "You do not understand. You obviously do not. Just now, you see, just now I told a very handsome young man that I had to 'go outside and fart,' because you are standing in his window, making a gigantic ass of yourself, which—mind you—I don't really mind, but if he sees you he's going to come out here and beat the living hell out of you. Do you understand? Do you understand the level of aggravation you've worked me into? Do you?"

"So... You're not in danger."

"Go. Sit in the car." At that she turns from me and cracks the door, slipping back inside. I turn as well, back into the burnishing wind, ducking my head into my shoulders. Holding my collar up around the back of my neck I start across the long distance Meredith left to her car. Heavy and cold, the wind is so loud blowing past me that I don't even hear the truck coming down the   driveway until it's right in front of me and I look up to catch the driver's face. And he looks to see mine.

I've no idea what my expression looks like, but I suspect it might be a mirror of his as he draws past. Locking eyes there's a quiet, dumb look about him, his face almost pulling back into a acknowledging smile, his neck almost cocking to give that timeless guy-to-guy-nod that strangers exchange and then that dumb look succumbs to an even dumber look—this the look of a man trying to place a face—before the dumbness contorts into a look of sudden, pointed rage. He seems lost for a moment as to whether he should stop, or accelerate, the truck shrugging briefly as he struggles between the two, but I've already straightened and turned to come toward him, which seems to spur him into action.

The truck jams up, rattling to a stop before the house. The brother—I forget his name, the one who is not Todd—lands on the ground, yelling at me, "I'm gonna fuck your fucking face up, fucker…" and jabbing his finger in the air. I'm marching toward him when his finger drops and he turns, leaning into the bed of the pickup.

Todd's on the front stairs already. That same dumb expression that was on his brother's face is now on Todd's. Trundling down the steps, Todd's started yelling now, too. Meanwhile, Not-Todd has risen out of the bed of the pickup, armed with a stout length of two-by-four.

He's still paces off when he starts bringing back the board and, though it's a short chunk—maybe four feet—it's long enough so that it takes him time to bring it around and, in that time, I launch forward. He doesn't even have it all the way cocked back when he realizes what it is I'm up to and has to start forward with it.

I think to grab the board, but it's too late, I'm already well inside his swing and instinct has taken over, and I give him a deep uppercut to the groin. The board and Not-Todd uncouple grace-lessly, Not-Todd contorting into a ball before he's even hit the ground and when he does land, it's with a groan so full of pathos that it almost makes me puke.

Todd seems stunned by the quick dismissal of his brother and pauses involuntarily. Again, it is simple instinct (not poor-sports-manship) that directs me, when I take the invitation and cuff him good across the eye. He folds just as awkwardly, if less nauseating-ly, than his brother.

With both boys handily dispatched, I march past them to the house, where Meredith has emerged. Reaching out to take her in my arms as she rushes toward me, I notice, too late perhaps, that the look on her face doesn't seem particularly gracious. In fact there is something distinctly menacing in her look; not unlike the look that dawned on Not-Todd after his dumbness waned. I'm only starting to lower my arms when she punches me solid, right in the sternum, knocking the wind from me. I fall forward, clutching my chest.

"I told you to wait in the damned car, you dumb asshole," she yells, passing me by as I try to rise to my knees, still clutching my chest and gasping.

I struggle to my feet. My chest hurts, my knees, too, from where I landed. Todd, I can see, is going through—more or less—the same thing, struggling to get to a half-crouch and, seeing me coming back towards him, he raises a hand to me. I shake my head with a 'not-even-if-I-wanted-to' sort of defeat.

Meredith's car whispers to life behind me and I think, 'Well, now I'm fucked.' Because even if Todd and Not-Todd and I are all brothers-in-pain, all losers-of-the-great-fight now, soon they'll be recovered and I'll be the poor sad-sack stumbling down their road alone. On their island. A little nerve twinges at the fact; especially now, seeing Not-Todd fighting to rise. We lock eyes and there is not-one-iota of that camaraderie I found in Todd's gaze. No, he's just straight-up-pissed.

I stumble to him and put my boot on his ass and push him back over, looking up as Meredith pulls alongside me. She doesn't say anything, doesn't look at me when I climb in. She lays on the gas, the tires spraying gravel over the two.

Meredith's face is bright red as she tears down the Rutter's driveway and out onto the road. "When I say stay in the car, Barry," she says through clenched teeth, "What do you do?"

"I thought you were in danger," I say.

Her jaw comes unlocked so that she can yell at me, turning to face me, her temples and neck knotted with worked-up-rage, "When I say stay in the car, Barry?! What do you do?!"

"Stay in the car," I say meekly. This seems to loosen a valve in her and the redness in her face dissipates and her breathing starts to even out.

26

As the woman working the ticket booth counts out my money, I ask, "I was wondering if you happened to see my aunt? She was hoping to make the earlier boat. She looks kinda like a pineapple with purple hair."

With my tickets and change laid out on the counter top, the cashier levels a dreary glance at me to say, "Drives a Prius with a boatload of stickers on the backend?—she made the seven-thirty." Her eyes narrow. "Mentioned you, too. Nothing about being her nephew; said we should keep an eye out for you—that you have a temper and a police record."

I shake my head. "That doesn't sound like my aunt. Probably a different person, altogether," I say. "Probably two entirely different people, you're thinking of. Thank you." Cleaning off the countertop and stuffing the change and tickets into my pocket, I make a hasty escape from the bright little office.

The wind calling up from the ocean tries to hold the door open after I've passed through and I have to lean in to it to get it closed again.

Out on the asphalt lot before the ferry terminal, Meredith's lined up in the queue—a couple of cars already pulled up behind her. The lot is half-full: cars left by islanders doing chores on the mainland.

Beyond the angled rows of parked cars, Ray's standing at the water's edge, looking out over the channel to Vinalhaven. Lodging my hands in my pockets, and turning my face down from the wind, I cross through the lot to him.

He has that look in his eyes again—that distant, vortical look. But when I follow his gaze out toward the island across the bay, whatever it is out there that's fixed his attention is lost to me entirely. The channel is almost empty, just a few fishing boats left at their moorings, bobbing and rocking in the quick chop. All the leisure boats of summer residents have been retired for the winter, so the channel is open and gray, windswept and foreboding and the island across doesn't look a whole lot different; those bare trees all gray as the water, the houses all dark, so if I unfocus my eyes, it's almost like there's nothing out there at all.

When I fail to find whatever it is that has Ray so mesmerized, I tell him, "I'm worried about you. I'm worried the Witch won't give up on finding you... On whatever it is she has planned for you."

He nods, but it's hard to tell if he heard me at all. The wind tugs his hair and his jacket and it's strong enough and cold enough so that I don't know how he can stand staring into it like this. I have to squint to keep my eyes from stinging. I ask, "What was in the box, Ray? What was she was trying to do to you? Do you know?"

Still gazing out to sea, he says, "She's probably right about some things. There are things you don't know. Things you refuse to acknowledge..." Continuing to stare silently out I feel, for a moment, that he's forgotten about me again, before his posture goes slack and he says, "Out on that island all those years ago, do you remember what I said when you found me? Do you remember that?"

I try to remember. I remember him helped up onto the boat and laid out on the bench. I remember the coarse, wool blanket they laid over him—a blocky black and beige plaid. I can't remember him saying anything. I ask, after a moment, "Was it about Suzy Trask?"

A smile breaks over his face. "Did I ever tell you about Suzy Trask?"

"What was it, Ray? What was it that you told me?"

He's still smiling. I can tell he's thinking about nipples, about nipples the size of tea-plates, his smile is so wide now. Still, in his eyes there's that disconcerting dreariness; an abiding and cavernous sadness. He says, "She had the biggest areolas you've ever seen..."

"I think it may be better if you stay out here for a few days. Just until I get this business with Nevers wrapped up. Just a couple days and I'll come back for you. I think I'm the reason the Witch found you in the first place and if I can just finish up this stuff with Nevers..." I trail off, saying, one last time, "Just a couple days," before turning from the wind and letting it push me across the lot, back toward Meredith's car.

In the Civic, Meredith and I are quiet. She might be angry— maybe that's why she's quiet. But, I'm hardly thinking about her silence, scarcely concerned for what reasons it may or may not exist.

The ferry comes to dock and there's a bustle of activity from the ship's hands before it disgorges onto the island. A wash of cars and a small throng of foot traffic pours past and, I'm not thinking about the Witch, or Nevers or Josephine. I'm not thinking about Todd Rutter or his dumb, nameless brother. I'm thinking about Ray. I'm thinking about how, since pulling him off that desolate island twenty-five years ago, not a day's passed without my having seen him. Not a day's gone by where I've missed him, not a day without feeling like he's looking after me. I twist around, to look through Meredith's side window for him, but the cars in the parking lot obstruct my view. He needs to stay, I tell myself. I tell myself, it's the only way I can keep him safe.

Our line of cars starts forward. I watch out the window to black waves throwing themselves up against the pylons as Meredith directs the car up the ramp. The warbly reverberations of the ferry throb through the car, through my guts.

Twenty-five years, I think. Twenty-five fucking years. Most of those, I considered him the only friend I had. Looking passed Meredith now, all silent and sour, I can't help but wondering if, maybe Ray is the only friend I'll ever have.

The window beside my face is clouded over with the ghost of my breath by the time the engine below bellows more lowly and the ferry grumbles away from the shoreline. Fumbling with the door handle, I push out into the wind. Behind me I catch Meredith's voice, "Barry?" in the moment before my ears are filled with wind's shrieking.

Squeezing between the cars parked along the deck I try to move quickly, but am hamstrung at every advance by side mirrors blocking my way. Cutting between the bumpers of two trucks, to avoid a narrow gap up ahead, I clobber my shin on a trailer hitch. The surge of pain stops me while I grit my teeth and reach down to try and wring the ache out of my leg. Launching myself forward again, the ferry starts to slow and turnabout.

I stand, perplexed a moment, as the islands circle the ship, North Haven and Vinalhaven changing places, while the ferry rights herself to cross the bay. Running back in the direction I came, by the time I get to the chains at the stern the ferry has started forward again. The island's already distant. The water's black and there's no one waiting at the launch.

"Ray…" Tears pool in my eyes from having hit my shin.

"You okay, Barry?" Meredith lays an arm around my back. I can't help the way I lean into her. It's reflexive.

Back in the car, she studies me quietly awhile, while I lean up against the window, the cold glass pressing against my face. She asks me again if I'm all right. When I say that I am, we're quiet for a moment. She says, "You standing in that window, waving. That was the funniest thing I've ever seen. You looked like you were signaling an airplane—I can't believe Todd didn't notice you."

"I'm sorry you had to tell him you farted."

She grumbles. "It was an adventure. You were right. It was what I needed. Shake the dust off."

"Yeah?"

"Next time I ask you to stay in the car, though…"

27

With the day fallen away, Meredith sits at the kitchen island, strands of hair glistening where they've come free from the towel around her head. For the last hour the only regular sound has been the dry note of pages turning. Now and again a reflective "Hmm," from her.

The silence makes plain Ray's absence.

With Meredith lost in Josephine's diary, he's all I can seem to think about. The loneliness feels like a burdensome artifact—like something heavy piled on my chest, something so heavy the only choice is to suffer it. Two days, I think, trying to comfort myself. But, it's hard to believe that voice in my head.

Flipping over a page, Meredith says, "I don't know. It's hard making any of this into anything... I mean, we're looking for authenticating details, right? This whole thing's... She never mentions her father at all and if he doesn't know anything about her... I'm just not sure where to begin..."

"What about your conversation with Todd?"

"Well," she says, "Keeping in mind it was a short conversation... A very short conversation... And for the record..." she says.

And I already know what's coming, so I don't even bother letting her finish, before parroting, "When you say stay in the car, I..."

She cuts in, "You stay in the car. Very good. It's nice to know I only have to treat you like Pavlov's Dog and eventually it sticks. Just think: if I'd told you to stay in the car twenty times before we got into his driveway, you might not have that bruise on your chest."

I pull open my collar to check the bruise. It's big and dark and perfectly centered on my sternum. A bull's eye. Looking up again, I ask, "Anyhow...Are you at least convinced that T and Todd are the same?"

"I am. He told me about an argument that Josephine mentions in her diary—over a Christmas gift he got her... It seemed like he was really in love with her. That he was hurt when she left. It's kind of heartbreaking..."

I nod. "He's a fucking murderer."

"How's being hurt make him a murderer?"

"He's bummed out that she left, not that she's dead. Sounds like a murderer to me. Sounds like a Grade-A psycho. You said, she wrote in there that he pushed her? Fucking violent psycho, right there..."

"So speaks the pot."

"What the fuck's that supposed to mean? I'm not violent. Unlike some people. Who punched me in the chest..."

"You asked for that," she says. "...And, nonviolent?! You?! What kind of alternate reality are you living in? You're the most violent person I know. In and out of jail..."

"I can be not violent and not be nonviolent."

She looks confused for a moment. "Do you hear yourself when you say things like that? Do you hear the words that are coming out of your mouth? That's complete nonsense, and illustrates exactly my point," she says. She's folded the book closed now, leaving a finger in to keep the page. "How many fights have you been in?"

I shrug. "I've never pushed a girl. Never would."

Mockingly, she echoes my gesture. "Was that a shrug—I've never thought about how many fights I've been in, or a shrug—I've lost count?"

"Never thought. Besides, I'm not a lady. Men get in fights. That's what men do."

"Not all men get in fights, Barry."

"You're right," I say. "Some men are ladies."

She shakes her head, "You're saying, you can't be a man unless you fight—that's what you're saying?"

"You said it—but, sure, I'll agree."

"That's dumb. Ghandi was never in a fight..."

"And he wore a dress: ergo, a lady."

She frowns and the moment of silence afterwards makes me think she's conceding that battle. "How about Stephen Hawking? Perhaps the smartest man in the world—bet he's never been in a fight."

I shake my head, "That's not fair, he's paralyzed." She just looks at me. "Okay... Fine... Stephen Hawkings—mostly robot. He's exempt."

"Stephen Hawkings is not a robot."

"He's got a robot voice, he moves around on wheels like a robot..."

"Not all robots have wheels..." Shaking her head and batting her eyelashes extravagantly, she says, "What about Ray? Ray wasn't a fighter."

"Sure he was."

"No. He wasn't."

"With somebody. Sometime. Sure he was. I'm sure of it."

"I'm telling you he wasn't. Not ever. Look at me, Barry." She shakes her head. "Not once," she insists. I look away again, unconvinced. "But, we're not talking about him, are we? We're talking about you. You are a violent person. Let's talk about how many fights you've been in, I'm curious. Let's think on it now. Go through the list."

"I can't do that."

"Okay—can't because you don't want to think about it, or can't because the number is just too exponentially large to even contemplate? Are we talking, like a super-computer-sized-number here?"

"I'm not violent," I say.

"Are we talking about a fast-food-chain 'served' sized number here?"

"Leave it," I tell her.

"A number quantum physicists might encounter?" She looks at me.

Arms crossed, I stare into the middle distance where a bulb of blue-white irritation has started heating my face—a little eyelet of anger growing like a scratched rash.

"How many commas does this number have? Here, I'll make it easier on you: can you tell me, just a rough guesstimate now—no need to tack it down too tightly—the last time you got through a whole year without a fistfight?"

The light from the lamp on the end table is a throbbing, astringent on my growing, pulsing rage-rash. Beading into shards through the filter of my wetting eyes, the lamplight cuts into me like glimmering, rainbow teeth.

"A season, maybe? A whole fall, perhaps without throwing a punch?"

"Just zip it, already," I yell, finding myself rising. But rising alone is only the start. I'm moving, feeling the air wash by my limbs, cooling my boiling anger.

Suddenly my hand is spiked with pain and I've stopped, heaving. Sucking air like I've risen up from below the sea. My head's clear again.

"What the fuck, Barry?!"

I look down. The room is a little darker. The floor is littered with porcelain shards and a toppled fabric shade and spatters of blood. Another drop lands from the cut on my fist. Meredith's eyes are wide and settled on the mess on the floor. I say, "I'm sorry."

She's quiet until after I've cleaned up and taken out the bag with the dead lamp in it and come back inside to find she's moved the lamp from beside the recliner to the table by the couch and she's sitting with her legs wound up under her, her face back in Josephine's book.

Taking my seat again and looking at the new lamp in the old lamp's place, I can't help being a little bothered by the unspoken accusation in the rearrangement. Without lifting her head, Meredith says, "So, now it's a lamp and a box of Cheese Bitz, you owe me. Break anything else and I'm putting you out on the street. Seriously."

The guilt dulls a little after that.

After a little quiet, I return to the thought I was approaching before the lamp started that altercation with me. Thinking aloud, I say, "Does she say anything else about him being abusive?"

She gives me a sidelong look before dropping her head back to the diary.

"You said something out on the island, about the 'T' code. About keeping secrets from prying eyes… What if he was worse than what she wrote? What if he was really violent," I say and mention of the word 'violent' colors my face a bit, a fresh twinge of guilt twittering up.

Laying the book on her thigh she says, "What are you doing, Barry? Do I need to remind you: we're not solving a mystery. That's not what we're doing. We're coming up with a plausible story. We're inventing a story to tell Nevers so that he'll pay you and go away. Right? That's what we're doing. Not playing Sherlock Holmes…"

"What if Todd…"

She points at me aggressively. "Don't. Don't even start on that. Do not tell Nevers that. Outside of the fact that we have absolutely no evidence…"

"He pushed her."

"That's not evidence."

"That he's proven himself to be a violent person in the past, I would say, most certainly constitutes evidence."

"You throttled my lamp, dip-shit. Using the same threshold of proof—for all I know, you killed her."

"That's not fair."

"It's not fair that you ruined my box of Cheese Bitz either, but it happened," she says. "Do not tell Nevers anything like that, okay? I'm gonna need you to promise me."

"Okay," I say, finally. "What do we tell Nevers, then? What's our story? Where is Josephine?"

"What do *you* tell Nevers?" she says. I keep looking at her, even after the pause has gotten strained. She shakes her head. "I'm out. I broke into that house with you... I told a cute guy that I farted for you. That's it for me. I'm done..."

"Come on. This is it. Our last adventure. Besides, I need you. You're the actress, Meredith. You're the only one who can sell this..." She gives me a look, like she knows I'm stroking her ego, but also like it's working.

28

~

From his wicker chair, Nevers looks back and forth between Meredith and me, his eyes scrimshawed red. Burning above a spilled-over ashtray, his cigarette and the hand holding it seem forgotten. The room is saturated with smoke. Moving toward the window, Meredith asks, "Could I..."

Seating her with a commanding gaze, Nevers asks, "You are?"

"His friend."

"He doesn't have friends—who are you, really?"

"His brother's girlfriend. From a long time ago," Meredith says. "And his friend."

Nevers nods, "Forgive me my third degree; I'm worn out on troupes. Priscilla and her wunderkind turned out to be utter failures."

"Failures? They've given up?" I try to keep any ring of jubilation muted from my voice.

"I suppose so. Priscilla said that they couldn't find her—Josephine—that she can't be found." Grimacing, he says, "That she isn't a ghost at all... Poppycock. She's still in my head, I can feel her, even as I take refuge here, in this dreadful inn. She's crossed the borderline somehow. She's searching for me. She hasn't found me, yet." He says, "But, here you are. So you must have something for me. Let's hope it's worth my money. It pains me to acknowledge this, but it seems you're my remaining hope." The strain is dug deep into his face. He's wasting away here, in this smokey room. He looks thinner, his hair thinner, his voice thinner, his skin thin and ashen. After a hungry, final drag from his cigarette he quashes it into the ashtray, butts and ash spilling over the edge, onto the table.

"Let's get to it, then" I say, worrying—imagining poor Josephine caught in the steamer trunk.

I nod to Meredith and she starts in, "Josephine, your daughter, dated a boy in high school named Todd Rutter." She pauses, waiting for some sign of acknowledgement from Nevers, which he refuses to offer. She continues on, after a moment, "Two weeks before she went missing, they broke up..."

Nevers cuts in, "I must admit, I don't much care for these extraneous details. I have to wonder, what's this got to do with with my problem?"

"Do you not want to hear about your daughter?"

"Whatever it takes to get free of her; that's what I want. If it takes me listening to teenage melodrama—fine, so be it. But know, I have a very limited tolerance when it comes to my time being wasted..."

Meredith looks at me.

"Is this what it will take?"

Meredith opens her mouth, but I'm the one who speaks. "Yes," I say. "You need to hear the story and then we can work on exorcising her. Then, we'll get you free from her."

"Fine," he agrees and looks to Meredith again, gesturing irritably for her to continue and lighting another cigarette in the spare moment before she does.

"The night she disappeared, your daughter attended a party near her house. Todd was also there. He was having a tough time with the breakup, apparently, and making the party... uncomfortable, shall we say, for Josephine. So, without saying goodbye, she snuck off, starting home along the coast, following the shore. She slipped.

"She hit her head on the rocks and fell into the water. Her passing was quick and painless, but the current dragged her body out, far from shore. That's why she was never found. That's why her soul got lost," Meredith says and goes quiet a moment before finishing, "And she wants to be found..."

Sighing dramatically, Nevers shakes his head, effectively cutting her off.

Meredith looks at me, dropping the narrative and I ask Nevers, "What's wrong?"

"I don't buy a bit of this. While Priscilla's opinion was disappointing, at least it rang of truth. This hokum, however..." he says, continuing to shake his head.

Lowering her tone into her 'actor's range,' and gesticulating broadly, Meredith doubles down, "This, I can assure you, sir, is far from hokum. This is what happened. This is Josephine's story..."

Like a kid on the verge of a tantrum, Nevers won't stop shaking his head. "No. No. I don't buy it. Not a bit of it. That isn't the sort of story that makes a ghost. No. No. I'm afraid not. Ghosts, you see, are born of great trauma, of injustice. Ghosts are made by murder, by wickedness. Not trifling accidents, clumsiness, teenage soap-opera..."

Hurrying to save our performance, I say, "There is some evidence that foul play could have..."

Meredith cuts in, "How do you deign to know anything at all about the workings of the spiritual realm?—about what does and does not motivate a ghost?—when you have right here," she says, thumping me hard on the bruise on my sternum. I wince. "The authority on the matter." Now, turning to frown at me, she says, through her teeth, "As for any notion of foul play?!"

"Deign," he starts to challenge, shouting over her. "Deign?!" His face is scarlet and wound up knotty with veins, but it's the healthiest he's looked since we sat down.

I interject, "Mr. Nevers, please, allow me to apologize for my assistant's presumptions..."

Beside me, Meredith mutters sourly, "Assistant's presumptions?"

I continue on, "We're still quite unclear about what—exactly—transpired on that rocky shore. Josephine seems to feel that she fell, that she tripped on the rocks and fell quite innocently, but keep in mind, if she was pushed from behind..."

"She wasn't pushed," Meredith says.

"Or, even, if she'd been given a roofie... There is very compelling evidence to suggest that you're right and that foul play was..."

"There's no fucking evidence, Barry," Meredith chimes in.

"Having shown himself to be capable of violence in the past, my assistant and I both agree, it isn't out of the question..." I continue on, over her.

"...Completely out of the question..." she says.

I keep going, "...That he may have poisoned her. In fact, Josephine has her own suspicions in that regard..." I sit back, having run out of anything sound to say, having run myself right out of breath. Meredith's face is all scarlet now, to match Nevers', but he seems satisfied, at least.

"Yes," he says, as though Meredith's every argument was utter silence. "That's the making of a ghost, I'd say. Poison..." Looking to the ceiling, pondering it a moment, muttering again, "Poison…"

Meredith, in spite of the cold grip I dig into her thigh, keeps going, "Let me interject—that that is not what happened." Looking at me now, she says, "We talked about this and murder is just not…"

"It's a good point! It's a very good point," I cut her off. Turning to Nevers, I say, "What my assistant is getting at is this: we felt it best not to disclose our suspicions to you, given how little evidence we have against Mr. Rutter. If you were to feel that Mr. Rutter was due legal inquiry, we could, in no way assist you. Do you follow me? We're simply here to exorcise Josephine from your dreams. Agreed?" I look at Meredith nodding encouragingly, but her face is stony in spite of it's ruby hue.

"Yes. Of course," Nevers says. "I have no interest either, in digging up old bones, only in putting them to bed. This murderous Rutter boy can be left with the torture of his own conscience as far as I'm concerned, mine is clear."

"Very good," I say. "I think we can continue, having settled that matter." Meredith still looks quite pissed; the look on Nevers' face is unaffected—his gray pallor now restored.

Clearing her throat Meredith says, "Regardless of how she fell. Regardless of the fact that she insists she tripped, innocently and that there was no…"

Nevers face starts souring up again and so I cut her off, "Meredith!"

She takes a breath and sighs, lowering her tone to say, "… She's been waiting for you to start looking for her, Mr. Nevers. She's been lost at sea, waiting for her father to find her…"

"Wait! What? I have to hire an expedition party?!" he demands. "Plenty of people searched; no one found her. Why do I have to take my precious time... And I suppose it's going to be terribly expensive... These things always are..."

I clear my throat. "Nevers. She wants you to find her—symbolically. Metaphorically. That's what we're here to help you with tonight..."

"I just want to be able to sleep," he says, slumping to the side.

"That's what we're working toward. I assure you."

I turn off the lights and open the shades, so that the thin light from the street pours in, tossing angular ghosts through the smoke in the room. We set candles out, lighting them as we go and arrange ourselves around the crowded lobster trap table. Getting the man to part with his cigarettes takes more effort than I feel it should but, finally, when he does, we link hands and I instruct Nevers to look down at the shadows playing around the base of the candles and I tell him, "I will now ask the ghost, Josephine, to enter the body of my assistant." I start chanting incomprehensibly for a moment.

When I've stopped my performance, Meredith makes a great show of hers, as though trying to upstage me, twitching and spasming and groaning and then, very suddenly, going rigid and quiet. I have to fight back the nervous laughter quaking in my throat when I ask, "Josephine, are you with us?"

Meredith says, gravely, "I am here."

"Josephine," I say. "Is there something you'd like to tell your father?"

I cringe in the little pause that waits on the other side of my question, because I know Meredith is debating whether or not the ghost, Josephine, will remind us all that she was not murdered. Relieved, I sigh, maybe a bit too loudly, when she says, in a fiendishly high-toned voice, "Daddy? I miss you. I waited so long for you to come and help me." Why Josephine has a British accent, I couldn't say, but Nevers seems unbothered by the detail.

We are silent, Josephine, Meredith and I, while we wait for Nevers to respond. When he does not, even after I've squeezed his hand, I say, "Mr. Nevers do you have something you'd like to say to your daughter, now that she's here with us?"

"Please stop bothering me. Go bother that boy who poisoned you, but leave me alone."

In the same quaking, silvery voice, Meredith says, "No one poisoned me, I simply tripped. It was an accident."

Nevers raises his head and I quickly warn him to look away. When he complies, I rush to say, "You may have been poisoned, Josephine. We discussed that. Todd Rutter..."

Maintaining the ghostly voice, but speaking up, she says, "Todd's a nice boy... Things didn't work out with us but that's no reason to go pointing fingers..."

"You may have been murdered, Josephine..." I insist. "But, I really think we should move on from this point now and work toward bringing you to your deserved peace. That's why we're all here. Don't you agree?—Josephine?"

Still ghostly and even louder, she insists, "I just want it made clear: I was not murdered. There was no poisoning. I simply slipped. Maybe I drank too much. High school girls do that sometimes. With inexperience, they don't know their limits..."

"You could have been pushed, too—we discussed that..."

"What is going on here!" Nevers demands. His eyes have opened and he's lifted his head.

"Don't look at her," I warn again, but the warning is too late and ignored.

Letting go our hands, Meredith gets to her feet. "I told you, Barry, and you promised me..."

"Meredith," I say, letting loose of Nevers as well and getting up with her, pleading, "Please, just sit. We can get through this..."

"No." She shakes her head. "No. I never should have agreed to this. This is just messed up and I shouldn't have agreed to it..." Turning to Never's she says, "Good luck with your... craziness," and turning to me she finishes the sentiment, "Both of you."

At the top of the stairs she refuses to face me as I continue to plead, "Meredith, please..." She stomps down the stairs.

When the door cracks shut, and Nevers and I are left alone, he looks at me slowly. "Is Josephine still here?"

"No," I say. "I do believe she left."

Covering his face he leans forward, resting his elbows on the coffee table. Whether or not he's crying, I can't tell, but his posture and the slight shudder of his shoulders suggest that he is. I hit the light switch and cross the room to him. Depressed and deflated and already anxious with money-worries again, I dump myself into the wicker seat across from him. We're quiet awhile.

"Is all lost?" he asks.

I blink—once, long and deep, searching the darkness behind my eyes. Finally, I manage to tell him, "No. But, I'll need another advance."

29
~

Waiting at the bottom of the stairs—when she sees my face—Ajna's smile fades. "Can no one take this man's money? He offers it to the world in his open palm and no one takes it."

"What happened to Priscilla and Children of the Corn?" I ask.

She shakes her head. "An honest palm reader—who knew there was such a thing? She tells me that he is troubled. That he is not well. That she won't take his money. Says I should be ashamed. I'm hopeful you're not suffering the same overabundance of conscience."

Passing her by, toward the door, Ajna falls in step beside me. "I'll take his money, I'm just having a tough time closing the deal."

Halfway through the lobby, Ajna takes my elbow, redirecting me to the kitchen, hissing, "This way." I let her guide me, but in my pocket, my hand tightens around the five hundred bucks Nevers doled out. A sheen of sweat's broken out over my forehead. She says, "You have a plan, though? You're not giving up on me, are you?"

"No, I'm not giving up."

Crossing through the kitchen, I'm almost to the exit when she stops me with a cold question, "Forgetting something?" I blink.

She holds out her hand. I think to argue, to protest. But, then, remembering how much it cost me last time, I hand the money across. She counts out two piles onto the countertop. "I was worried you would hold out on me."

"No, no," I say. "I just thought we were waiting until the end of the whole transaction to, you know, settle up. May I make a phone call?"

Handing me my stack of bills, she returns to the countertop to recount the other pile, telling me, "The Inn charges long distance fees for all out-going and in-coming calls..."

"I just gave you two hundred and fifty bucks..."

"There is also a minimum charge of five dollars per call..."

"Never mind," I tell her.

A fragile, frigid rain has started falling. It's cold, dark and I'm feeling alone as I shuffle down Union Street, and maybe that's why the lit windows of the library seem so inviting and I veer off down the long, paved path to the front doors.

Inside I'm confronted with the calm quiet of the place. There's a desperation in my aimlessness as I wander down the chasms between the book shelves in Nonfiction, running my finger down the spines, like an old man dragging a cup across jail-cell bars. Dread over prison is persistent now. With my freedom in quickening contraction, I'm distracted with worry about what will become of Ray when I'm gone. And worry about Ray, in that future context, starts a spiral of worry about him in the here and now. It makes me impossibly lonelier thinking of him out in that icy rain, out on the island, vulnerable and alone.

Running out of aisles to pace, I find a free computer and sit and've only just gotten past the screensaver when a librarian approaches from the side, saying, "You have about ten minutes before we close, sir."

She's already moving on to the next patron. "I just sat down."

"Ten minutes, sir," she says, but it's hard to tell if she's talking to me or the next guy down the line.

"Would you help me with something, then?—just very quickly?" I ask.

"I need to let people know that we're preparing to close. I'll come back when I'm done."

"By then it won't be ten minutes anymore."

"I got him, kin," a voice chimes from beyond the privacy screen and there's Drew, all of a sudden, standing up and collecting a bag and a notebook and stepping around to help me. The librarian thanks him and starts off again while Drew pulls a chair up beside me.

"Jesus Christ, are you fucking following me?"

"Keep the f-bombs a little quieter, if you don't want to be asked to leave again," he suggests. Putting on a smile, he waves off the librarian, who's stopped midcourse to level an eye on me. "I'd keep the tone a little lower, too, for that matter, Cookie."

I lean toward him, whispering, "Jesus Christ are you goddamned following me, kid?"

"That's a little better, I guess," he says.

"Do you live here?—every time I come here, you're here."

"I've seen you here once," he says. "Do you wanna spend the next eight minutes going over my library schedule, or was there something you needed help with…"

"I need to find out about that Nevers girl…"

"You don't need a computer for that. I can tell you all about it." He shrugs. "But—seeing how that's a conversation we can have anywhere—how about we have it someplace else. Let's meet at the Electric Company in an hour. You can buy me a beer and some fries."

"I can, can I?"

Back outside the rain has picked up, but the Electric Company isn't far and it's warm inside and I'm happy Ajna left me with something in my pocket, so I order a beer and then another and, halfway through my third, Drew shows. Saddling up next to me, he says, "I prefer a light beer."

"How old are you?"

"Old enough," he says. But, when the barman comes down, he makes us move to a table away from the booze, because Drew obviously isn't old enough to be up on the stools. Reseated, off in a corner, I gripe for a moment about losing my warm seat and Drew says, "I could leave…"

"…Had to pull that 'old enough' bullshit… How old are you, anyways?"

He smiles. After a moment, he says, "You know, whatever you and my mom have between you, that's between you guys. I don't want you to think…"

"I don't 'think,' so let's just move on. Whatever she's told you, it isn't true. None of it."

"What exactly do you think she's told me?"

"No idea. But it isn't true. None of it. And I don't want to get into it," I say and we both go quiet, leaning out while the waitress drops off Drew's cola and a pile of fries.

When she wanders away, Drew throws a wad of them into his mouth and, intermingling his words and chewing, says, "You're going back to jail soon, right? She says you've been in and out."

"Yeah. That's right."

"She told me I should stay away from you—that you're better off left be."

I nod. "I guess I'd agree with her on that account, too," I say, and I steal a fry from his plate.

"So, tell me—what is it you think she's saying that she shouldn't be?"

"Nothing," I say. "Nothing. I'd say she's spot on about everything. Never mind that I said anything at all."

"But, you were thinking something that you thought she'd told me. I'm curious as to what that would be; what it is you think she's telling me."

"Let's just get to the business at hand: Josephine—I want that story."

"Okay—why you so interested, anyways?" he asks, pushing the hair back from his face.

"Why you interested; why I'm so interested?"

"Just like to know what the info's gonna be used for if I'm the one volunteering it, I guess. I caught you crashing that party. So, I guess I just wanna check on your intentions…"

"Let's just say it's business. Let's just say there's an interested party and leave it at that," In his silent, deliberate chewing he looks me over, searching my face. I say, "It's my business opportunity, understand? There's no room for other parties here. So, don't think about trying to hone in on it. Your mother already jerked me out of a good deal of money."

Raising up his hands he says, "I'm not trying to bite your paycheck, kin. I just want to make sure I'm not encouraging a stalker or anything…"

"A stalker? What the fuck are you talking about—a stalker? Who the fuck would I be stalking?"

His eyes narrow, but he shakes his head and says, "Okay. What do you want to know?"

"The story…"

"What'd you mean the The Story?"

"What do you mean—what do I mean? You're full of shit—aren't you? You don't know anything about Josephine Nevers... I'm not paying for those goddamned fries; I'm not paying for that fucking cola, if this is all you have for me."

"I know a lot. I just don't know what you want to know. That's all I'm asking: what do you want to know, you crazy dickhead."

"I want to know what there goddamned is to know. I wanna know the story," I say and when the dumb look still hasn't washed from his face, I say, "How about when she went missing? How about that? How about that fucking story."

"Oh. Okay," he says. His expression settles away. He gobs his mouth up with fries and starts chewing, looking out to a shadowy corner of the ceiling.

"Oh, my God." I lean back. "If you have something to say, just fucking say it."

"Okay, so she went missing, right," he blurts out. "She ran away. People freaked out. I don't know what you want me to say about it..."

"I want to hear what happened."

"Nothing. Nothing happened. They put her in as a missing person and a few days later she shows up in Portland..."

"Shows up? What does that mean—shows up?"

He shrugs. "I dunno. She was shacked up with some bozo down there. She'd just taken off and not told anyone..."

Rubbing my forehead, bunching closed my eyes, it takes me a moment to compose myself so I don't reach across the table and throttle the dopey, little douchebag. When I open my eyes, I keep my voice cool to say, "I am not buying you those fries. That soda, it's on you, 'cause I'm not paying for that, either."

"What the fuck, Cookie..."

"Don't call me Cookie. You obviously don't know about Josephine. You're obviously as big a liar as your mother is."

He stops chewing, his face gone serious. He says, "Don't say that about my mom. And don't you call me a liar, either. And if you know so goddamned much, why don't you tell me what happened to her."

"No one knows. If you knew anything, you'd know that much. She's gone and certainly dead."

"Dead? She's not dead."

I shake my head. "Lies. Fucking lies."

He's almost laughing now. "She's not dead, Caveman. She owns an antique shop, up in Belfast..."

"Bullshit," I tell him and I start saying, "I saw her ghost myself..."

"Her ghost? Holy shit, kin. You are unhinged."

"I saw her..."

"Wait, Caveman—was this out at her mom's house, at that Halloween party?" He stares a moment, his face cracking into a big grin. "That was a costume, kin. That was a costume at a costume party. Did you not notice everyone else there was dressed up, too?"

"Bullshit."

He laughs openly at me now, looking around for someone to share the joke with. "I swear to God—she was born on Halloween. Every year her mom throws a huge bash for her birthday. People come from all over to go to that party, up from New York City, even. I met a guy from Zanzibar there. I think it was Zanzibar. It's a big deal, I know—I've worked it the last couple years. Make good money handing out vittles."

"Vittles?"

"Hors d'oeuvres and champagne. Listen, Caveman, I'll take you there, to her store. I got tomorrow off. I'll take you up there. You can ask Josephine yourself about how she died."

"Bullshit," I say again.

He just shakes his head. "You buy me the fries, pay for gas tomorrow, buy me a pack of smokes and I'll show you Josephine Nevers isn't any damned ghost."

"Bullshit," I say one last time. But, when the check comes I pay it and tell him, "If you're taking me for a ride on this, I'm gonna take it outta your ass." When the waitress takes my money away, I tell Drew, "And don't even think, for one fucking second, that there's room for anyone else in this business deal, okay? You get a tank of gas and a pack of smokes and that's your end and I don't want to hear, at any point, ever, that you feel you deserve more than that."

He just stares at me, frowning, unimpressed, before he says, "Whatever."

"Not whatever."

"Okay. Whatever."

30
~

When I see the purple Prius hiding in the alley off Union Street—
before giving a breath to consider the consequences—I sneak into
the shadows beside it. Unscrewing the nozzle cap from one of the
tires, I open the valve with my thumb nail, showering my face
with sour, rubbery smelling air. I'm gleeful at the mad hiss.

The tire's half-slumped to the pavement when a voice stops
me, "Mr. Cook, you do seem determined that I have you arrested."

Smiling grimly, I pull my thumb away to look up at Priscilla.
Tomothy's at her side and neither of them seem amused.

"What is it you think you're doing? I needn't even ask. We all
know what you're doing."

Standing, dusting off my hands, I tell her, "Just checking the
pressure. Looked a little overfull to me. That can be very unsafe…"

Priscilla sighs, crossing her arms. "You see the position, I'm in,
Mr. Cook? You see the position that you put me in? I understand
you're a troubled man. And, while I don't wish for greater misery
to be visited upon you, I can't have you about constantly

tampering with my car, either. Do you understand the position you put me in?"

Shrugging, I suggest, "You could just leave town; pack up your shit and move along. That might solve the problem altogether."

"Have you spoken with Mr. Nevers?—you do understand that we're no longer in his employ?"

"I'd heard that," I say.

"Then why? Why is it that you persist in so clumsily tormenting me?"

I look her in the eye. "You know why."

She nods. "Raymond."

"Until you leave and I know that he's safe…"

"For the benefit of your beloved, you understand, I have no intention of leaving the matter of Raymond unresolved. So, you're forcing me into a position where I must call the police on you."

Looking at the tire, Tomothy says, "It's just the one. He didn't even puncture it…"

"Didn't have a knife…" I say, but no one seems to hear.

"That's not the point, Tomothy. Mr. Cook has already told us —demonstrated ad nauseam—that he's no intention of stopping this behavior. And, if we hadn't come outside, he would have emptied all the tires, you can have no doubt."

"But he didn't. Besides, he looks emptier than the tire. Let's buy him dinner; a truce, so we can talk. What'd you think?"

"I think we should have him arrested. But, if we're ruling that out…" Priscilla says, "And there's no other course."

Tomothy says, "Not the Rockland Inn, though. That Ajna Canth is a crook."

Returning to the Electric Company, Tomothy explains how Canth claims her corned beef hash to be homemade, while anyone can tell that it's from a can. "I mean," Tomothy spouts between mouthfuls torn from a Rubin sandwich, "The potatoes were cut to the size of pepper corns. That isn't homemade. You can't even do that with a normal kitchen implement..."

I nod. "You should see how she treats lobster."

Tomothy gives himself over to a big, theatrical shiver. "I'd hate to imagine."

Priscilla barely eats. I don't eat at all. I'm full of beer and she refuses to buy me more. In lieu of dinner I get a show—Tomothy's appetite is a spectacle; boundless and off-putting. He hangs over his plate, his strangely avian neck lunging and retracting as he bites and swallows, content with very little chewing.

"To business..." Priscilla says, "Where is our friend, Raymond?"

"Gone."

"Gone?" Tomothy says, pausing in ravaging the sandwich to look at me wide-eyed. "You don't mean—gone?"

I make a little gesture, a fluttering of my hand and repeat, "Gone," as though to illustrate that he'd wafted off into the ether.

"Hiding him from us," Priscilla says to Tomothy. After a moment, she she digs a photo out of her purse and pushes it across the table to me. Picking it up, the image it holds is instantly recognizable, unmistakeable. Hiding my surprise, I shrug and push the picture back. "She lives in Belfast. You can drive up there and see her if you like. I don't know if she'd welcome you. She wasn't very interested in speaking with us. She harbors quite the wealth of resentment toward her father. You don't seem as surprised as I thought you would…"

"I figured it out already. Probably before you did," I say casually. "Plus, I did see you on the beach with her in that costume."

Priscilla cracks a little smile. "Quite the getup. I'd imagined that you thought she actually was a ghost, the way you were acting," she laughs. "I guess I assumed you to be quite the rube. I should have given you more credit."

I feel my face coloring. "Yes. Definitely more credit. She wasn't interested in…"

"No," she says, nodding slowly and closing her eyes. "He's a very sick man. Very confused. Distanced from reality. Mental illness, I'm sure you know, doesn't just effect the afflicted. Its shadow tends to fall on loved ones. I can't blame Josephine for trying to insulate herself from it. Though, I'd hoped to get her to go and see him; help him put his 'ghosts' to rest." Priscilla shakes her head. "She wasn't interested." Sighing, her voice takes a sharper tone when she says, "I suppose I shouldn't be telling you any of this; I'm sure you'll use it to manipulate the man…"

Tomothy, through a mouthful of sandwich, says, "I don't want to hear arguing over a matter that's already past." Looking at Priscilla he swallows and says, "And that doesn't concern us any longer. We're no longer in competition, madam. We may disagree with Mr. Cook's motivations and methods, but if, through his means, he can provide Nevers with some newfound peace…Well, I hardly see the harm…"

"It's unethical. That's the harm, Tomothy," Priscilla says. "It puts our whole profession in a poor light."

Taking another bite from his sandwich, Tomothy says, "Let's move on. Let's talk about the real issue that brings us together here and now: Raymond. You say he's gone, but..."

"Gone," I repeat, stubbornly. "So what was Nevers' argument with the photo?"

"I take it, from your sly attitude, that you still intend to bilk the man," Priscilla says.

"Bilk isn't a word I'd use."

"It's analogous with cheat," Tomothy volunteers.

Priscilla, turning to him, says, "I don't think it's a question of elucidation, dear."

"I don't have any idea what that word means," I say.

"Perhaps I'm wrong, then," Priscilla mutters.

"Priscilla," Tomothy scolds. "To elucidate is to make something clear, Mr. Cook. Can we get back to the issue of Raymond?"

"It's fine," I say to Priscilla. "It doesn't matter what you think of me. If you think I'm stupid or a thief. You're a thief, too."

"In the eyes of most civilized peoples theft requires the procurement of..."

I clear my throat over her. "You two are every bit as shady as I am. Just because I'm a thief doesn't mean I'm dishonest. There's nothing dishonest about taking when you need. I never make people believe something that isn't true... You tell people you have access to some other plane of existence..."

Tomothy says. "But, Mr. Cook, your brother..."

"My brother's my brother and none of your goddamned business..."

"You're afraid of the gift you have," Priscilla says. "It terrifies you, because it reminds you—more than death—of life. Life scares

192

you, Mr. Cook. That's the cause of your hardships..." A little pit of anger radiates in Priscilla's eyes and, at this point, I can still recognize that that anger isn't hers, but my own. "Explain to me how what you're doing isn't sheer grift."

"Nevers decides whether I'm giving him what he wants. He came to me. I didn't ever tell him I was some bullshit psychic."

Priscilla smiles; there's not a smudge of good will to it. "What do you think the Chief of Police of Rockland would say about what you're doing?" After my silence, she says, "Because I've spoken with him about you." When this statement, too, fails to illicit a response from me, she asks, "What do you think he'd say about your letting the air out of my tires? Breaking my headlamp?"

"Priscilla," Tomothy whispers. "This is the wrong way."

Ignoring him, she goes on, "Perhaps you'd like to talk about Raymond, now, in that greater context."

"Priscilla..."

"Fuck you," I mutter bitterly. Getting up from the table, I turn and go to the door, because I know if I stay, I'll end up ringing Priscilla's fat, prickly head free from her wrinkly, stupid neck.

The cold air outside takes me instantly and I follow the streetlights down the road but I don't get far before Tomothy's shadow catches up alongside me. He stops when I turn to him. A little dab of thousand island dressing hangs from his chin, unnoticed.

"Please, Barry," he says. The dressing on his chin shimmies almost imperceptibly when he speaks, before falling off, onto his shirt. "Priscilla shouldn't have treated you like that. We have no intention of calling the police on you. I hope you know I won't stand for it. In spite of whatever shortcomings you may have, I am a great admirer of your gift." I simply blink, continuing to look at him. He blinks as well and holds the peace a moment longer before he says, "We need to find Raymond. We need to find your brother, before it's too late."

"You can't find him. You won't ever find him. He's mine and I won't let him go."

"Barry, you're not saving him. All you're doing is prolonging his anguish…"

I stare undeterred, staring as though the challenge in my eyes is a physical thing, heavy and hard enough to push him back; to push him back down the block, away from me, to push him back around the corner, down the cold asphalt street, to the Prius, to shove him and the Witch in, and propel the car, on it's mushy wheel out onto the road and far away, out of state, out of New England, down into the gray, shapeless and unseen reaches of a countryside that must exist beyond. Away from Ray. "He's mine," I repeat before turning away.

31

Within moments of pulling away from my house, Drew's smirk starts chafing me. Every time he turns his attention from the road to inspect me, the smile seems to get a little more comfortable, a little deeper-set in his face. "All right," I finally say. "What's the fucking joke?"

"We're going to Belfast, not the Arctic circle, Caveman," he says, laughing.

I am bundled up superabundantly. A layer of thermal underwear and sweatpants stuffed into my Carharts' makes me look like, overnight, I blossomed voluptuous-lady-thighs. Compressing my torso, a t-shirt, a flannel, a heavy wool sweater, and a sweatshirt, makes the canvas jacket overtop pull tight as a sausage casing. It's uncomfortable and awkward battling it, so I don't fight the jacket, instead letting the layers of fabric hold my arms weirdly away from my body. I tell him, "I don't have any fucking heat."

The smile slips away and he goes to quietly watching the road.

"And when did you get the impression it was okay calling me Caveman?"

The smirk plays briefly again when he says, "I could call you Pop."

"What the fuck..."

"It was just a joke, kin. Relax. How long you been outta oil?"

"It's not a fucking joke, though, 'cause it's not funny. You see —that's the defining nature of a joke: humor. Fuck," I say, looking down at the floorboards of his Crown Vic. "I wouldn't have offered you a whole tank of gas if I knew you were driving this goddamned boat. What's this thing cost to fill, anyways? How full's your tank now?" I ask, leaning over to examine the gauge.

"Don't worry about it—if you're so worried about it..."

"Don't worry about it? What—so you can come back at the end of this deal and tell me I still owe? Only, I'm sure by then it wouldn't just be a tank of gas you'd be asking for. I'll fill it, thank you. I just want you to know: I ain't happy about it."

"Jesus, you make yourself a hard person to like." He fumbles to light up a cigarette and cracks his window, smoking silently and leaning toward the vacuum of the world rushing by. The cab gets cold with the window open. The chill from my house is frozen right into me and I just can't seem to get free from it. I wish, for a moment, that I'd brought a blanket with me. He says, "If I'd known you were gonna be such a dick, I wouldn't have offered to take you up..."

"And if I'd know you were gonna harp on this Pop bullshit, I wouldn't have agreed..."

"Nobody's harping," he says. "It was a joke, Caveman. Just a joke. If I'd known you were gonna have a conniption over it, I would've kept my mouth shut."

"Maybe you should have. What's your mother saying, anyways to get that bullshit into your head? We messed around once, like twenty years ago and..."

He cuts me off. "First of all, kin. That's my mom, and I don't wanna hear about it. Secondly, I'm nineteen and last time I heard, it really only needs to be done once, biologically speaking, to, you know, make someone. But, to answer your question: my mother doesn't say anything about it." He takes a break from watching the road to suckle his cigarette and give me the once-over. "Look at us. We look like brothers."

"All white people are gonna look a little bit alike. That's biology. Fucking genetics."

"What—are you a racist or something?"

"I'm white! We're both white! How the fuck am I gonna be racist against whites? I'm just saying, all white people kinda look alike."

"Seems a little racist to me…"

Taking a breath, I go on to say, "Let me tell you a few things about myself, kid, just to get these delusions un-lodged from your impressionable, young brain. I have no money or anything of value. I haven't so much as wisdom to share with you, my man. Not so much as that. You have literally nothing to gain by pretending you're my offspring. Nothing."

"Let's just drop this. You're kinda pissing me off."

"Agreed," I say. After the air in the cab's gone astringent, I tell him, "Smoking's bad for you."

"Holy shit. Call the papers."

"It ain't a joke. My Uncle Ernie had emphysema—it's a shitty thing to see. Say nothing about having it yourself. Couldn't climb two stairs without losing his breath."

"Here's a deal: I don't call you Pop, you keep your opinions about my habits to yourself."

"Deal," I say. A length of road passes in silence. I say, "Ran out of oil sometime in the spring. Didn't seem like that big a deal, at the time. The days were getting warmer and longer and I just put off getting it filled." I shrug, looking out to the gray world passing by. "And I owe a little to the oil company. Not a lot, just enough so that I can't ever seem to get it together."

"Aren't you worried about the winter?"

"Of course I'm worried about the goddamned winter. I'm worried about the fucking sun setting."

By the time we've passed by Lincolnville Beach and turned off Route One into Belfast and Drew pulls into a parking spot on Main Street, the air from the vents has warmed me enough so I can lose the coat and the sweatshirt.

Across the way an awning adorns the front of a stubby, brick building. *J Nevers' Antiques and Oddities* is stenciled onto the green fabric. Rolling a twenty out from my dwindling wad of cash I toss it up onto the dashboard. I say, "Gas and smokes."

"You haven't even seen the ghost, yet," he smiles.

"Let's just say, I got a feeling you're right."

He's already stepping out onto the sidewalk. Something in the speed with which this is all taking place is suddenly nerve-wracking. I have to spill right out, to catch the same break in traffic that he does.

Slipping into the store behind him, I try to compose myself while a bell rings and the door latches closed at my back. So certain for so long that Josephine was dead, I'm stupefied by that trademark-mischievous smile that greets me from a few paces away. I look off, pretending a tarnished cellulose comb in a display case has nabbed my interest.

Drew just keeps bounding on toward her, announcing brightly, "Hey, Josephine."

Now, I really do look at her. In spite of Drew's familiar greeting, perhaps due to it, Josephine looks confused. Missing the cue,

Drew just continues on, swaggering to the counter and saying, as though they are the tightest of chums, "Hey, this is my buddy, Barry."

I force a smile and raise my hand.

She smiles back, before returning her attention to Drew, clearly struggling to place who he might be. She says, "Good to see you?" Drew nods enthusiastically and an awkward lull settles over the shop. "Were you guys looking for something in particular?"

"Barry..." Drew starts spouting.

I seize him by the elbow, dragging him away and telling her, over my shoulder, "We're just browsing..."

"What the fuck, Caveman," Drew starts in as I push him around a corner. "I thought you wanted to meet her..."

Tightening my grip on his arm, I shove him forward and shut him up with a hiss. We come to a stop at a dead end guarded by a horde of hideous, antique dolls. The store is clean and modern, in spite of it's wares and, unfortunately, offers no dark corners in which to hide. Even where I've lead us, as far from Josephine as possible, we're still clearly in her sight; looking over my shoulder I find her watching us through the failed blind of a shelf littered with figurines. I give a smile and nod before turning back to Drew.

"What the fuck is wrong with you?"

"Easy. Easy," he says, pulling my fingers free from him, brushing off his shirt, as though my greasy hand left a mark. "What's the problem, Caveman? I thought you wanted to meet her."

Turning back, over my shoulder, I find Josephine's given up watching us, returning her attention to a magazine opened on the countertop. I reel a little. Clapping Drew on the shoulder, I say, "I do. I can't just rush in here and... Listen, I just need to work it at pace, okay? I didn't expect you to run in here drooling and panting like a dumb fucking dog."

"Fucking dog..." he mutters, dusting his arm again, trying to loosen the wrinkles my grip dented into the fabric.

"Go look around. I'll get you a treat later," I say.

He frowns. "Don't talk to me like I'm a dumb fucking dog."

"Good boy," I tell him and pat him on the head and he wanders off muttering.

I start pawing through things, winding my way back to the front desk. There's a stack of suitcases piled up that smell of cement dust. A display case holds tin toys and the wall behind the register is mounted with taxidermies—old, dead animals, whole and in parts. The most peculiar is a pair of bunny heads, mounted side by side on the same walnut placard and when I'm close enough, I can see the brass tags below the heads: etched in curly lettering, one cute cranium has been named Jules and the other, Verne. My attention is drawn again and again to Josephine as I wander closer, trying not to look at her.

Off, at the other end of the store, I cringe at Drew's voice shrilling up, "How much is this?" He's holding up a bronze statuette of a bull dog wearing a beret with a big Holmesian pipe jutting from its mouth.

"There should be a tag on it. Check the base..."

With Drew distracting her, I take the opportunity to stare more carefully at Josephine. The troublesome little girl in the photograph has grown into a striking woman. It's no wonder Todd had a tough time letting go—what man wouldn't?

Having found the tag Drew barks out, "Jesus!" and sets the dog back quickly with a clunk.

"All prices are negotiable," she says.

"Five bucks?"

Josephine frowns. "What's the tag say?"

"A hundred and thirty..."

"Five's a bit on the low end… Was there someone special you were shopping for?"

I creep closer to the embankment of glass display cases closing her in, as Drew says, "My mom's birthday's coming up. I'm just struggling for ideas, kin…"

"There are some nice, well priced pieces in the case over here…" she moves to another counter and Drew and I congregate at the case, while Josephine points out some earrings to Drew. Smiling up at me occasionally, I can't help staring at her. It's alarming being so close.

"I like those," Drew says and she pulls out the pair, mother-of-pearl set in tarnished silver. She lays them on the glass top.

"How long you had the shop for?" I ask, finally having constructed the beginning of a conversation.

"About two years," she says, smiling briefly before returning her attention to Drew.

"You're young for the antiques market."

"I'm not for sale…" she shows me her smile again before she says, "People say I have an old soul…"

"Me too. He's out on North Haven, though." I laugh awkwardly, a spark of worry about Ray flaring up. In the stale moment afterward, I say, "Just kidding."

She seems confused, but smiles generously.

"Say—you're from North Haven, aren't you?" I ask and she shows me the smile again, but it's started looking a little wary. "Listen, I had a great relationship with my dad, okay? That said, you know, there are plenty of people I'd love to fuck with. I'm just that kind of guy. You hear what I'm saying? Now, this may seem a little weird…"

"It's already a little weird, kin," Drew mutters inwardly.

I narrow my eyes. "I have a business proposition for you…"

Now her eyes have narrowed, too, and she's scooped the earrings back up. Taking half a step back, she doesn't say anything.

I smile widely, trying to reinforce that I'm not a threat or a creepy-weirdo, but from the way that Drew's hissing, "Kin?" I think I'm only seeming more threatening and creepier for the forced smile. I let it fall, and raise my hand and say, "Just a business proposition, that's all." In the skeptical silence that follows, I hurry to say, "It's not a sex thing..." She takes another step back, a full step this time, and I rush to continue, before I lose her altogether, "I happened to see you at your birthday party a few days ago. I gotta say, that was a hell of costume. A hell of a costume. Jesus, when I first saw you I thought you were a ghost. And I was wondering, if you'd be willing to throw that on for a private audience—I think you know who I'm thinking of, right? It wouldn't even be an hour. Ten minutes, fifteen at the most. Maybe just walking through the woods. You wouldn't even have to talk to him. Or down a beach, that could work, too. You know, if you want to fuck with your old-man, I'm your guy. That's all I'm saying." In her lengthening silence, I say, "Two hundred. I could pay two hundred in advance." When the silence continues, I rush to say, "Another hundred afterward..."

Her mouth tightens up. "You're that terrible con-artist. You're taking advantage of my mother's ex-husband, aren't you?" She shakes her head. "You oughta be ashamed..."

"...Two hundred afterward. That's four hundred total, just to mince around in that costume..."

"Get out of my shop," she says. "Stay away from me. And tell Davis to leave me alone..."

"You do know he thinks that you're dead? We don't have to play the vengeance angle, if that's not your bag. You could look at it like charity—freeing him from this curse he's got..."

"Leave."

"...So, that's a no to wearing the costume? Just checking... A no?"

"I'm calling the police..."

She's reaching for her phone when, raising a finger to chime in, Drew says, "I think I'd like those mother-of-pearl ones."

Pausing, pulling her hand away from the cellphone, Josephine smiles and says, "I think your mother will like that..."

I'm made to wait outside while they complete their transaction.

32

∼

Even with the bell chiming, even with the waves thumping against the side of the boat, the world seems abysmally quiet without Ray around.

Hooking my final buoy, I pull up the line. Yard after yard coils at my feet, where a deep, tangled-nest of rope is already piled. It hardly registers that the trap is empty when I get it onboard and fastened down with the others.

Since my meal with the Witch and her blonde little shadow, I can't stop myself from thinking about Ray. Worrying about him. Whatever the Witch has planned, that she's determined to find him is clear enough.

Sitting now, looking out over the great, swaying plane of the sea, I keep going back to what Ray asked me out on North Haven —if I could remember what he'd said when that blistery, stubbled man and his blistered, pink daughter had carried him up, onto the boat. I'd hugged Ray, held his rigid shoulders before the girl pulled me away and they draped him over with that black-plaid blanket.

He was quiet back then. For days, maybe weeks afterward, he was quiet. He'd follow me around. I accepted his silence as a side effect of the trauma of being out there for so long. It was awhile before he found his voice; awhile before I heard him again.

With all five of the traps stacked precariously high, it's a long ride from Rockland Harbor back to Marine Park in Rockport, where I put in. The trip goes on and on. I can't focus on anything, but I can't stop thinking, either.

At Marine Park, the warm morning has attracted admirers who stand, staring out to the calm sea. Some turn to watch as I take the boat into the ramp and ground it. Avoiding eye contact, I cross the parking lot to my trailer, picking it up by the tongue and yanking it back to the ramp where I wrangle it around and aim it down at the water. Unlocking the winch I pull the hook free, catching the handle at the bow.

It takes a few tries before I get the boat to settle up straight onto the rollers and then, it takes me a lot of pulling to get the trailer and the boat, laden with all those traps, free of the water.

Hefting the trailer through the parking lot, everyone in the park has given up on the view, to watch me trudge my load along. I keep my head high, looking straight ahead. It's hard work hauling the trailer and acting like I'm not everyone's entertainment.

The road down to the launch is curved and steep. Even without all the traps and rope and buoys, the trailer'd pushed me down the hill impatiently this morning. Now, with all that new weight piled into her, leaning hard forward, in the end, I'm just not strong enough to drag the load. The traps are too much weight. My feet slip and the trailer tugs me back into the parking lot. Quickly worked breathless, I give up, letting the tailer have its way.

I sit on the curb exhausted, defeated and lonely again for Ray. Even though I know he wouldn't be much help.

Though the crowd's mostly given up watching, I still feel caught in an awkward spotlight when a man, about my father's age crosses the lot to me. "I got a hitch," he says. "I'll tow you up the top of the hill."

He tows the trailer all the way home. Pulling in my driveway he says, for the fifth time, shaking his head, "Jesus, bub. I can't believe you drug that thing all the way down there."

The house is just as cold when I go inside as it was when I left this morning. Just as cold and, seen in the daylight, the house looks abandoned. Everything is dusty. The ceiling in the living room has a big crack running down the center that wasn't there before.

I try cleaning. The smell from the basement leaches up through the floorboards and, when I stop, looking over what work I've done, I'm discouraged to find that nothing looks improved. Finally, (after ten minutes, maybe) I give up and go outside.

Setting the traps and the boat out by the road, I make up *For Sale* signs and tack them up. In the garage, I find a metal trashcan and pull it out into the driveway, feeding it with junk-wood scoured from under the eaves. The can fills with flame and I stand close by.

With the Autumn sun warming my face, I work my hands into fists, trying to get them back from the cold. When I have feeling back enough to punch the numbers on my cellphone, I give Meredith a call.

"So, Josephine's not dead," I tell her when she answers. I can hear her breath over the line, otherwise she's quiet. "You're not surprised?"

"Honestly, Barry, I feel pretty bad about everything. I'm a little ashamed and I don't think her being alive really changes that. I think I'd like to just forget about the whole mess, put it behind me—chalk it up to some latent teenage stupidity I needed to work through."

"You won't drive me and Nevers to Belfast, then?"

"What's in Belfast?"

"Josephine."

"You're planning on harassing that poor girl." Watching the fire feast and turn at the sides of the trashcan, I'm quiet, trying to arrange an answer. Quiet long enough so that Meredith fills the gap for me, "I don't want to be involved in this anymore, Barry. I don't think it's good for you. Or Nevers. Or me. I think if you're interested in getting together a nest egg you just need to sell the house and that's all there is to it. When you want help with that, I'm more than willing... Otherwise... Bye."

The line goes dead.

I hold the phone in my hand a moment before hitting the 'call' button again.

"Do you need help cleaning the house?"

I sigh. "Yeah. I do. You're right."

In the time it takes her to come over, the flames sputter out so that all that's left, when she pulls into the driveway, is a trace ribbon of black smoke issuing from the can.

"Hobo party?" she says, without much humor, but then, when I bring her inside, she says, "Jeez, it's cold in here." And, when she's had a moment to look around, she says, "Let's get some lights on."

"There's no power."

"I thought you said..." She's quiet a moment. "Okay," she says, shaking her head. "No vacuuming. Do you have a broom?"

I nod.

"Then let's get a hot, soapy bucket going."

"Meredith..."

She looks at me. "No hot water?"

I shake my head. "No water. Period."

"Jesus, Barry." She walks away while I stand in the kitchen. The house rattles when the front door shuts. Through the window, I see her getting into her car. The engine purrs to life and pulls away.

Back outside I throw a chunk of rotted wood into the trashcan, but it's too late. The fire is gone. I sit in a lawn chair and hold my head in my hands. It's a nice day—dry and, now with the sun well into its afternoon arc, it's not so cold out of the shade.

I'm shocked when Meredith pulls back into the driveway, stepping out of the car to chide me, "This isn't gonna happen if you're sitting around." I stand up like a soldier going to attention. "What's with the boat and the traps?" she says.

"Taking advice. Selling 'em."

"Don't sell the boat, Barry. Don't sell the traps."

"If I sell the house, I got nowhere to keep a fucking boat."

She walks out to the street and takes the signs down and balls them up and comes back, throwing them into the trashcan, where they manage to find enough heat to wither up black and ashy and catch a little flame. She says, "I'll hold them for you at my house. Can't get rid of things you need. That doesn't make sense. Just get rid of what's hobbling you."

I help her carry bags into the house, bags of cleaning product, several gallon jugs of water. We start in on the kitchen.

The floor's a completely different color when we finish scrubbing and move onto the living room. There's something arresting about the smell of bleach in the cold. Wiping the dust away, everything looks different; new. After the living room's cleaned the two of us separate—she disappears into Ray's old, time-capsule room and I start in on the mess around my bed. When I pause and listen I can hear the bristles of her brush working the walls and the floor, the slap of water in her bucket when she drowns the brush.

"I think Pa worried that I resented him," I say. "And he was right. I did resent him. It wasn't fair of me, I get that now. Pa didn't send Ray away. Ray volunteered. Thing is this; Ray wasn't ever just a brother to me. He was the person I wanted to grow up to be. When I thought about what a hero was, I wasn't thinking about a cowboy from some movie or an astronaut I saw on TV; I was picturing Ray. You know?"

In the other room the sound of scrubbing stops. I listen to the silence a moment. It's perfect. So perfect it's almost possible to think that Meredith isn't there. That I can be honest. That I'm alone. I feel lonely.

"The whole reason Ray got on the boat that night was that Pa was sick. He had a flu... If Pa hadn't been sick... Who knows, maybe he'd have gotten lost instead of Ray. Not that that would have been any better. If that had happened, I probably would have resented Ray, instead. Who knows?

"We were always getting calls in the middle of the night. Of course, it was never good conditions. No one wants a sea-taxi when it's daytime; calm seas, no wind. It's always nighttime. Always windy, choppy. Cold.

"I remember waking up when the phone rang, knowing with no doubt at all, that it was bad news. That the whole thing was drenched with bad. Just dripping trouble.

"I got out of bed and went downstairs. Pa was already half suited up, but Ray and he were in the hallway and Ray was saying, 'No, you're sick. You shouldn't go. I'll go.' He didn't get a lot of argument from Pa. You could see the sickness in his face; he was all sweaty and it was a cold night. It was right before Christmas, you remember.

"I got in the middle of them and I start saying that neither of them should go. That it's bad news and that whoever goes isn't gonna come back... I'm just begging them not to go. Twelve years old and crying for 'em not to go. I get this look from Pa—I'm acting like a kid and there's no place in our house for that... Leukemia got mom, so who's around to take care of a kid?"

I tell the waiting silence in Ray's room, "I mean, you were a housecleaner sometimes, a cook sometimes, a baby sitter and everyone appreciated it, Meredith. I know Dad did. But, you weren't a mom. You couldn't be. You were half-a-kid yourself and trying to do whatever you could to keep Ray's attention. I get that. I think I got it a little bit back then, too. Maybe a little bit.

"Anyways, he suits up and goes. He goes and I knew it was bad. All night I knew it was bad. Laying awake, staring into the darkness, I knew it was bad. I could hear the wind outside. When the sun came up I kept watching the wall. Didn't get up to go to school. I watched the wall and listened to Pa's alarm clock screaming from the other room. Listened to Pa downstairs, making calls, listened to the desperate murmur of his voice. Called the Coast Guard. Called his fishing buddies. Anyone with a boat. Called you, I guess, so you came over to watch me while he went out to help search. You kept telling me it was gonna be alright. That they'd find them. But, it sounded like you were asking me. I didn't tell you what I already knew; what I'd known all night.

"Days went by and the Coast Guard searched and Pa stayed out and came home and went out again and he never once talked about my tantrum—about begging Ray not to go. To this day we've never talked about it. Like it didn't happen.

"Days went by and the Coast Guard didn't find anything. Not a thing.

"And this is the part I'm always asked about and never answer:

"I woke up and there's Ray, over my bed and his eyes are like waterspouts, sucking everything up into a gray sky. He doesn't say anything, but I know to follow him. So, I follow. Out, onto the road, out into the night. Down to Marine Park, where I got into Uncle Ernie's boat and found where he hid his key.

"I don't think Ray was with me the whole time, but I was following him nonetheless. Out into the night. Out into the sea.

"They'd been drinking, this rich old guy, Paul Andrews, and his daughter, drinking in Rockland and they'd missed the last ferry back to Vinalhaven. That's why they called for the taxi. So fucking stupid. Such a fucking waste. Ray picked 'em up. Almost to Vinalhaven, they got off course, ran up into a rocky spot, cracking the hull. The boat filled up quickly.

"It was windy and choppy and dark and trying to get them into the life-raft, Ray slipped and hit his head and fell into the water. That man, Andrews, managed to get Ray back on board, I guess, but it was too late."

I snort. My throat feels thick, but I keep going, talking through my achy throat. "He managed to get the raft to a little, rocky island out in the middle of fuck-all-nowhere.

"I came on 'em, right at dawn, all blistered, windburned. Frost-bit, dehydrated from days out there, exposed. They were in bad shape, but even though I'd known for so long, I couldn't help with Ray. Not when I saw him. They did that. They got him on-board and covered him over with a blanket, even though they both could've used it more than him."

I take a breath. "This is the thing. Everyone says what a fucking miracle it was, my finding them. Not for me it wasn't. I didn't find who I was looking for. And everyone says, what a gift I have, that I saved their lives." I shake my head. "It isn't a gift. It wasn't ever a gift. You can't make people listen. You can talk, but you can't make them hear.

"And, at any rate, I didn't save them. Ray saved them. It was always Ray. Just like always, I was in his shadow. Only, now it doesn't offer me anything. It isn't a break from the wind. Or the cold. Or the sun."

Meredith's come into my room. She sits beside me on the bed and lays her hand on my back, looking into my face while I look down at my feet.

The day's turned to dusk before we finish cleaning. Looking over our work, I notice Meredith's nose twitch. "It still smells," she says.

When I show her the basement, she slumps down, to sit on the stairs, a look of defeat settling over her. "You need a dumpster, Barry."

"I don't have money, Meredith. If you brought me and Nevers to Belfast..."

"I can't help you with that. I won't."

I nod my head.

33

The first snow of the season sifts down from the sky; tiny, wet wads smacking the windshield to vanish immediately. The road sizzles beneath the tires. The heater hums. The radio is on, tuned so low the music is unrecognizable, just a muted drumbeat: thump-thump. But over and above it all, intertwining with it all, Drew talks steadily. "So she's wrapping up her GED now; trying to get into that community school in Thomaston." He laughs. "...A lot of time in the library these days, oh boy. But, I'm wicked proud of her..."

No one is paying attention.

Beside me in the back seat, Nevers seems to be deteriorating by the moment—fading closer to nonexistence with every breath. Had I not seen the stages elapse, I might not believe him to be the same man I met at the Rockland Inn, just weeks ago.

"Have you been this far up the coast, yet?" I ask. We're nearly to Belfast now. "Nice country."

Drew keeps talking, straight forward toward the windshield. When his eyes wander up to the rearview and meet mine I look away, out the window.

It, maybe, isn't such beautiful country, at any rate. Beyond the shadow of Camden hills, there's not much to see: the tall trees on the roadside are stripped of any green, commercial lots cut up the landscape. Driveways and minor roads snake off into the distant woodlands. The sky is low, gray, heavy.

"Better in summer, maybe," I say. Lighting a cigarette, Nevers acts like he doesn't hear me when I tell him, "Roll your window down."

I can't stop thinking about Ray—imagining Ray, his gaze settled out on the water, his eyes gone gray and distant and growing more and more disconnected with every wave that gropes the shore, with every sigh of wind in his face.

He's pulling away and I need to get him—I'm anxious with the urgency of it. Even now, heading back to Belfast to earn the biggest paycheck of my life, all I can think of is Ray. I clear my throat, trying to settle into the business pulling us northward. "I'll need you to remember a few things when we see her."

Nevers suckles his cigarette, staring away.

"Window down."

He takes a deep draw and blows a pipe of smoke out toward the center of the car; the casual arrogance grinds on me. When a swell of anger starts rising up, I clear my throat, trying to suppress it. I start again, "There are some things you need to remember…"

Nevers doesn't look at me. After another lungful of smoke, he passes a bored gesture with his hand.

From the driver's seat, Drew starts coughing. "Put that window down, kin. Jesus, I can barely see the road." Nevers just keeps smoking. Rolling down his own window, Drew goes back to talking, the noise from the wind diminishing his voice to a meaningless drone.

"There are some things…"

"Yes. Yes," Nevers says. "Some things I need to know—so, get on with it..."

"Well," I say. "It would be nice if you'd fucking respond when I talk to you."

"I gestured."

"It's fucking rude, is what it is. Here I am, leading you around, taking you to find your daughter. Taking time out of my life when—you know what?—I have better things I could be doing. Better things," I say, thinking again about Ray; wondering what's the earliest ferry I can likely make today.

Mashing his cigarette out on the door handle, Nevers drops the butt to the floorboard and turns to me to say, "Let's get this clear, Cook. I'm paying you. You are my employee. I expect you to do your job quietly and without a bunch of bullshit." We lock eyes. "Jesus," he exclaims, turning abruptly away. "It's like an entire state populated by morons."

Meanwhile, Drew has stopped his chatter a moment to turn over his shoulder and say, "What'd you do with that butt, kin?"

"Eyes on the road, fathead," Nevers says.

"Seriously, kin. It smells like something's burning."

Sure enough, the cigarette has caught a stout blade of fire on an abandoned fast food wrapper. I tell him, "Stomp that."

"Don't boss me. I'm the one paying here."

"Kin, seriously," Drew is craned around to Nevers again.

"Watch the road, fathead!"

Turning back ahead, Drew barely gets the Vic out of the on-coming lane in time. The car shakes in the passing blare of a tanker-truck, horn booming and fading quickly behind us.

"You crazy dunce. Watch the road next time."

Kicking his legs out of the way, I push across the short span between us, and stomp out the little smoldering fire, all the while

Nevers is yelling, "Get off me, get off me, you brute," and I'm yelling to Drew, "Pull over! Pull the fucking car over!"

Drew's already given up the road. The car bounces, gravel knocking off the undercarriage as he ditches the car onto the shoulder. Before we've come to a complete stop, I'm out the door.

Catching sight of Nevers' face as I come around to his side, that look of casual indifference is gone altogether; he's barefaced-afraid, eyes wide. Moving quickly, he snaps down the lock as I reach for the handle.

I stomp to the woods beside the road, finding a fist-sized stone in the culvert. Drew's on my heels as I climb back up to the road with the rock in hand. "What are you doing, kin? What are you doing?"

Back at the car, Nevers is screaming through the window, "You maniac! Stay away!"

I straighten tall, bringing the rock up over my head. Drew's joined in the yelling now, too, screaming over Nevers, "Not the window, kin! Don't break the window! I got the lock, kin!"

The clack of the lock unlatching comes too late. The rock's through the window. From a perfectly transparent plane, it turns into a shower of tiny geometric droplets, Nevers ducking back just in time so the rock misses him.

I grab the door handle from the inside as Nevers shrinks away from me. With the door open, I lunge inside, getting Nevers by his jacket and dragging him out into the street. "Ow, ow," he complains as I pull him across the pavement.

Drew's behind me, again, pleading, "Ease up, kin. Ease up. He ain't worth it." I get a quick look at Nevers' face, all wound tight and gaping. It freezes me right up. I lose my grip on him, letting him fall back, onto the damp gravel beside the road.

Opening his jacket, I feel him down, finding his pack of smokes and taking 'em, holding 'em up for him to see. Once I know he's seen, I crush the box up in my fist and throw it away into the woods.

Behind me, Drew's surveying the mess I made. The window isn't quite gone. It's displaced—parts of it hanging onto the frame, limply hanging over the door, some on the ground at my feet littering the floorboard and the seat. "You killed my window, kin," Drew says.

"Nevers'll pay. Isn't that right, Nevers?"

He nods and I lift him by the lapels again and put him back where I found him and (like a good paid-man) swing the door shut for him. The flap of shattered glass squeaks like a mouthful of loose teeth when it flops against the door.

"Still wish you hadn't broken it," Drew says. Climbing into the front seat, I leave Nevers alone in the back.

On the road again, with the window gone, it's a cold ride, what remains of it. Nevers is silent, holding his jacket around himself, the side of his face all wet and dripping with snow.

"You should have thought about it when I asked you to crack the window," I say. He shivers and is silent, looking dead ahead. It's only after a few moments, driving again, that I'm aware of my bloody hand, the cut from Meredith's lamp is open again. "… Should have thought about it."

We're almost to the Belfast off-road when Nevers finally breaks his silence. "Just take me back," he says and, after I ignore him, he repeats himself.

"We're not your employees," I say. "Let's just get that goddamn straight. You're my client. And the only reason I didn't leave you a broken mess in that ditch back there is…" I can't think of a reason, other than the hot wave of embarrassment I felt from Drew seeing me out of control like that. "If someone asks you to roll down a window, what do you do?"

"Please, take me back to Rockland."

"No," I tell him. "We're finishing this, you and I."

He pinches his eyes closed. "I don't want to finish it."

"So what then, Nevers? What then? You chain-smoke yourself to death in the attic of the Rockland Inn, while Ajna Canth bleeds you of your every-last-penny? Is that it? Is that what you want—just to give up?"

"Yes. Take me back," his face is compressed horribly, half-turned from me, facing into the icy breath blowing in through the ragged-edged-window-hole. His hair is wet.

"No," I say. "We're finishing it. We're getting paid for it. Isn't that right, Nevers?"

Nevers hangs his head.

At the edge of the downtown block of lower Belfast, I have Drew make a wide u-turn and slide the Vic into a parking spot, a little ways up from *J Nevers' Antiques*. Nevers seems not to notice the sign or, if he does, it doesn't seem to resonate with him. My hand's started throbbing.

"You need to know some things," I say.

"Okay," he says. "Tell me what I need to know."

"You cannot interact with her, no matter what."

"Okay."

"She'll look older to you. Older than she did when she disappeared. That's just the way it is. Some ghosts' don't know better than to age."

"Okay."

"She'll look flesh-and-blood-real to you," I say. "As real as anybody on the street. That's 'cause you're family—that's how you'll see her."

"Okay."

"We're not going to interact with her. When we see her, you're gonna start chanting *Go away, ghost. Be free. Leave me be.* Okay? After that she'll disappear; it'll seem like she's just turning around a street corner. But, she'll be gone. Exorcised. You get all that? You got any questions, now's the time."

Nevers is quiet.

"Good," I say. He shivers and holds himself and leans forward to catch some of the heat blowing from the vents. The way the hot and cold pouring in through the back window mix, feels like water running over me, the way they swirl together. We wait.

It doesn't take long before Nevers complains, "Are you sure of this? Where is she?"

"She's coming," I say. "She might be slow, but she'll be along. Ghosts are bound by habit. It's like work hours for them; they stick to it…"

As though upon command, Josephine appears in the door of the antiques shop; closing it, locking it behind her and strolling toward us, down the sidewalk. Somehow, by crazed coincidence, she has dressed the part of a ghost: a white sweater, the knit loose enough so that it seems to sparkle over a gray blouse beneath. A light-cream scarf is cinched around her neck and looped over her head, falling down behind her and jazz-handing in the breeze. Nevers seems impressed. He gasps. "It is her."

"Oh no," I mutter as she keeps coming on.

I'd assumed she would cross the street at the crosswalk, but she hasn't. She just keeps coming on. "Oh no," I say again, quietly and I hurry to instruct Nevers, "Do not look directly at her. Look away."

I have hope for a moment, when her eyes fall on us and she pauses, that she'll turn and leave. Instead, she lurches forward again, coming around the car and leveling a cold, venomous stare on me before turning her attention to Nevers. Embarrassingly, he's begun chanting, "Ghost go away, be free and leave me be. Ghost go away, be free and leave me be. Ghost go away..."

He just keeps on chanting as she closes in, bending down, to look through the open hole in the glass. "What the hell are you doing here?"

Nevers keeps on chanting, the apparition of his breath breaking over Josephine's face. Somewhere in my gut, a big embarrassed groan starts unwinding.

"Next time I see anyone of you weirdos around my shop, I'm calling the police..." she looks at me and she looks at Drew, who's turned away from her, hiding against the glass. "Did your mother like those earrings?"

Drew nods quickly.

"Glad to hear it." Giving her father one last, cold look she straightens up and continues on.

Nevers is still chanting when I push the rearview out to track his daughter, walking away from us. She never looks back. When she turns, gone around a corner, gone from the rearview, I tag Drew on the thigh. "Let's get out of here."

Cranking the wheel, he sends the Vic into a squealing u-turn.

Out of Belfast, we're all quiet and I'm promising myself I'll never go back there again. Nevers is the first to speak. So quietly so that it almost can't be heard over the wind shuddering through the car, he says, "Did it work? Am I free?"

It takes me a moment, turning the question in my mind before I figure out what he's asking. "Yes. Yes. Of course it worked," I can't fight the smile on my face, the brightness coloring my voice. "Of course you're free."

34

It appears as though Nevers has annexed his room entirely from the clutches of the hotel staff. Makeshift ashtrays have sprung up on virtually every surface. A glass tumbler left on the end table looks to have been the scene of a small, intense fire. It's full of ash and the glass is blackened.

As though trying to mask the sour odor of old smoke, immediately upon entering the room, Nevers finds a pack of cigarettes in his nightstand and gets busy firing one up. Sitting on the bed, he smokes mechanically for a few moments, his gaze aimed off arbitrarily to the floor.

"The checks, Nevers," I tell him and he jerks up, reminded of my presence once again.

"I'm not…"

"I don't want to hear it," I say and start toward the dresser. "Where's your goddamned checkbook?"

"I'm not entirely convinced…"

Starting through the drawers and digging around, I tell him, "I told you: I don't want to hear it. Where's the fucking checkbook?"

"What if she returns?"

His checkbook is tucked beneath a wrinkled wad of khakis. It's one of those big ones, the size of an art book you might find on some asshole's coffee table and the cover's made of a supple, leathery looking plastic. I toss it on the bed below him. Eyeing it, where it landed, Nevers makes no move.

Looking up from the book, he asks "If she returns?"

"That wasn't the deal. We never discussed any money-back-guarantee."

"I'm not paying for a service you didn't provide…"

"You saw her," I growl, coming closer. The ash on his cigarette falls onto the comforter when he flinches. The coverlet looks like something salvaged from a home fire. It's sticky with ash and tufts of cottony filling poke up from burn holes. "I brought you to her…"

"I'm not so sure it was her…"

"You're kidding me. Of course it was goddamned her. Who else could it have been?"

He shrugs. "Priscilla and Tomothy tried a similar sort of trick."

"Goddamn it, Nevers. Write the fucking checks."

"How do I know…"

"Because you saw her! With your own goddamned eyes, you saw her! That's how you know!"

He blinks and goes to nodding a moment. Without paying attention to what he's doing, he reaches out and crushes the cigarette on the tabletop beside him, close to an overspilt ashtray. The cigarette keeps on burning as he shifts to collect the checkbook.

"Three checks," I tell him.

"Three?"

"Is there a goddamned echo in here? Your nightstand's on fire." He isn't paying attention to me. Bent over, opening the checkbook, he pulls a pen from where it was tucked along the binding. "Your nightstand," I say again.

The fire is weak and flickering, fragile. I watch it grow a moment before turning and going to the bathroom. Emptying the trashcan out on the floor, I fill it up under the tub faucet.

The fire's nearer the lamp when I come back in and, somehow, Nevers still hasn't noticed it. I wind back and dowse the table. Water splashes up onto the bed and across the wall, which finally manages to get the man's attention. "What the hell are you doing, you buffoon?"

"You're gonna burn the building down."

He goes quiet, looking at me.

"What is Ajna charging you for treating her property this way?"

"I'm sure there'll be a fee assessed."

"I'd say so." We stare at each other a moment. "I'd say you're gonna end up buying her a whole new hotel."

"My bed's wet," he complains.

"What's a broken car-window cost?"

"I'm not a glass technician."

"Call it a thousand, then. We'll just chalk that up to a being-an-asshole surcharge. Make it out to Cash. Then, I want two more checks to Cash, for five thousand each."

"You still haven't answered my question: what if she returns?"

"I did answer your question: I don't care."

"…If she returns?!" he demands.

"Have you ever thought, Nevers—have you ever considered—the root of why she's coming to you in these dreams? Has it occurred to you that, perhaps, the reason that you're having these dreams is that, maybe, you feel a little guilty about your lack of involvement in your daughter's life? Look down into your heart,

Nevers. Tell me that's not a little true. You feel guilty and you're lonely, you have no one who cares about you."

"I have plenty of people who care about me..."

"Who? Name one."

"You name one!" he says acidly. He's silent a moment. Looking at me, he finally says, "Names aren't important. We both know that."

"Sure," I say. Sighing, I turn away from him, hands jammed in my pockets, and sit on the edge of the bed. "You're very popular, clearly. Three checks, all to cash."

"What if she comes back?!"

I turn to him. "You have no guilt?"

He shakes his head, no.

"And you're not lonely?"

Again, he shakes his head.

"Then there's no reason for her to return. You're free."

He writes me the checks. And, after he's handed them across, he climbs under the covers. Before I get to the stairs he's snoring and, descending into the stairwell, I pause to hear him mutter, "No, Josephine, no..."

Maybe he deserves it. I let myself out into the hallway.

In the lobby, Sarah Goldstein eyes me from the front desk, giving me a cold "No," when I ask if Ajna is around. Taking one of the big checks and laying it on the countertop, I say, "Give this to her when you see her. Or don't. It's to Cash and, quite frankly, I don't care who gets it."

She slides the check off the counter without turning from me.

Drew's outside, his car still running when I emerge from the hotel. He doesn't look at the check when I hand it across, just smiles, folding it and tucking it away into his shirt pocket. "That's for helping out. And the window," I say.

"No worries," he says. "You need a ride anywhere, Caveman?"

"I'm just going down to the ferry terminal," I tell him and he reaches across the seat and pops open the door for me—even though the terminal's only around the corner. And, even though it's just around the corner, I get in.

We're quiet until he comes up on a light and we sit as traffic fills in the intersection and then a little while longer in the empty gap afterward, watching the traffic drift away down Union Street. I say, "I'm sorry about your window."

He nods. "It's all good, Caveman."

"I'm still not real keen on this Caveman shit."

"Pop, then?" he says and smiles.

"How about Barry?"

He nods. "I can work with that."

"I'm no kind of a father figure, kid. I got no wisdom. For my thirty-seven years I haven't made anything but a mess. I haven't ever done anything good."

We've gotten through the intersection, come back around Main Street, passing the Strand Theater. He takes a moment before he says, "Do you think, Barry, you're such a dick half the time 'cause your brother isn't around?"

"I'm not a dick."

"Yeah. You are. You should accept that. It doesn't make you a bad person. It just makes you… Well, a dick," he says. We're both quiet a moment—I guess, because he's right. "I told you about my mom going back to school, right? The thing is, she's kinda my hero. It's not like she's Super Woman or anything. It's just, with her around, I know I need to be a better person. Not 'cause she asks me to, but just 'cause I wanna make sure that she always sees the best part of me. You know? It just seems like you don't have anyone you're trying to impress and I'm not sure that's a good thing…" He takes the turn down the ramp to the ferry terminal, parking down at the bottom and I get out into the day, hanging in the doorway a moment. He nods to me. "I'll see you around, Barry. Be careful."

"Thanks, kid." I nod and shut the door.

I get myself a ticket for the last ferry of the day, even though it'll mean spending the night outdoors on the island. With my pockets filled with food out of the vending machine, I sit and watch the day eke away and wait for the ferry to come.

35
~

The day is long-done by the time the ferry rumbles in to dock on North Haven and, when the engine dies, the resulting quiet is like some new, extrasensory hearing—I'm suddenly aware of everyone around me, chatting and breathing, the rustle of clothing as they stand, collecting their things and queueing for the cabin door. I sit to sponge what last heat I can before rising to go out into the cold again.

Outside, a caravan of cars trundles through the parking lot, out onto the street—headlights flaring through the trees and fading away. When the last car has carried off the last passenger, the parking lot is surrendered to quiet darkness, just the light from the stars glimmering on patches of ice, on the metal guard rail that encloses the lot. The hiss of the wind fills my ears. The ocean booms.

Interrupting the sea's tirade, I yell out, "Ray?!"

I keep calling, hoping if he's close enough to hear that he'll follow my voice and find me. When he doesn't show, I start down the road, away from the ferry terminal. The wind and I move together, calling as we emerge from the village center. The wilds of the island wait right at the brink. Trees bow about the road and if there are homes around, they aren't lit and can't be seen and I wander on, continuing to call. The trees have demands of their own—creaks and groans and snapping—like a whole neighborhood shouting for quiet.

Eventually I stop, worried that I'm lost. I call out a few more times before turning back. The return feels quicker than the venture out and I scold myself for being a sissy and not going deeper into the island. It's been a few days now and Ray could have wandered anywhere.

Back in the village center, I'm shaky with cold, but I turn down toward the water anyway. Lights shine across the bay from Vinalhaven. There, at the edge of the ocean, I finally find him, waiting in the wind. His voice drums, "I'm here. Barry. With you."

Thump-thump, thump-thump, thump-thump, the ocean beats against the pylons.

"I missed you, Ray. I don't know why, but I had this dread that I'd lost you. That I wouldn't be able to find you."

He says, "I'm here. Right here."

Thump-thump. Thump-thump.

"I love you, Ray," I say and turn my back to the sea and head up through the lot to find a windbreak.

It's gotten late. Maybe it's gotten late, or maybe being out in the elements is exhausting. I find a spot out of the wind behind the ticket building. I curl up on the ground and try to fall asleep but, it's too cold to slip off. I lay there awhile, clenching myself into the tightest shape I can hold. Still, the cold winds in, up the cuff of my jacket, through the gap between my pants and shirt. And then the rain, thin and icy-cold, starts falling.

I try the backdoor at the building, but it's locked and sturdy, giving me only a bell like note and a sore shoulder when I try muscling into it. I circle around, trying the windows as the rain picks up. On the building-side facing the ferry, I find a high hopper window. Pushing on the frame as hard as I can, the latch breaks with a weak, plastic snap. I hoist myself up and slide down into the darkness of a narrow bathroom.

It's warm inside after I pull the hopper closed, warm in spite of the draft that creeps down the wall from the twisted window frame. After checking the lobby through a gap in the door, I decide that staying in the bathroom, even with the drafty window, is the best call.

"We've slept in worse places," I tell Ray and I lock the slide bolt on the door and get down on the floor. Leaning to the side, I wrap my arm under my head.

Sleep is slippery and shy. It comes and leaves so subtly it's hard to tell which direction it's headed from one moment to the next. I nod in and out, Ray watching me quietly from the corner. "I love you, Ray," I tell him. He doesn't say anything back, but I know he loves me, too. The smile on his face obscures the sadness in his eyes. Like he misses me the same way I miss him.

Through the window, the sky is lightening when the jangle of a bell jerks me awake. The rain has passed. The room is bright enough now to see everything dimly. Even so, it takes me a moment to get my bearings.

Out, in the lobby, there's the ringing of the cash machine, someone whistling while they ready the ticket counter for the day.

My shoulder and knee are stiff from the floor; it's tough getting up without letting out a groan. Standing on the toilet, looking out the window, I can see the ship's hands preparing the boat for the day. A string of cars has already lined up. A couple of old men are standing out, leaned into the bed of a truck, talking. I drop down from the toilet seat and cross back to the door.

The whistling has gone quiet. There's nothing to hear. Sliding back the bolt I crack the door and look out. It's a she—the same cashier who gave me shit the last time I was here. She's up on a stool, hunched down, filling in paperwork, her back to me. When she starts whistling again, I close the door and slide the lock back into place.

Like the needle's been pulled from a record, the whistling stops. Breathless and listening, I let a moment pass.

"Hello?" The door handle rattles. A moment later, the bell at the front door chimes.

Climbing back up on the toilet, I look out the window again. She's out there, the cashier, rushing across the parking lot toward the ferry. Hopping down from the toilet, I go to the bathroom door and get out into the lobby, scurrying through it, into the day.

The line of cars for the morning trip is already long, and the cashier's already at the head of it, flagging down a man on the dock. He's got a captain's hat on. They turn back together, lighting eyes on me, the cashier and the captain. Starting back across the lot, she raises her hand, aiming a finger at me and the captain picks up pace, starting by the row of cars, passing the first car queued up, which catches my attention—a purple Prius, the back bumper cluttered with stickers and out there, moving casually toward the car, is Ray.

I yell out, "Ray! Stop!" My feet are already moving when Tomothy slides out from the passenger side door, greeting Ray with a smile and a word I can't hear.

I yell again, "Ray!" running faster, at sprint now, forgetting entirely the cashier and the captain breaking the distance to intercept me. Tomothy must hear my yelling, he turns to look up at me, but Ray doesn't stop, doesn't turn, still trapped by whatever spell the Witch has him under. He keeps gliding toward the back of the car where the hatchback hinges open wide like the mouth of a snake.

I'm running so hard, I almost knock the captain over when he catches me. I push myself off him, my fist already curling closed.

"Easy. Easy, fella," he warns me, with a hand on my chest. "What's the problem?"

I knock his hand off and try stepping around him, but he's big and won't be moved around. "Listen, bub," I start saying, but more ship hands have starting gathering down at the dock, summoned by my commotion. A few men have been drawn out of their cars as well, watching me.

"You're Barry Cook, aren't you?" Looking into the man's face, I don't recognize him at all. "Paul Andrews is my father-in-law."

Looking past him, Tomothy's got the trunk closed up now and I can't see Ray anywhere. I just catch sight of the blonde boy slipping back into the car.

I tell the captain, "I need to speak with that man there," pointing out to where Tomothy had been standing. When the captain looks, the spot is empty.

Turning back to me, he says, "Why don't you move along. Take a walk."

"He broke into the office." The cashier's just behind the captain now, insisting, "You can't just let him leave."

"Was the cash drawer tampered with?" The captain's asking her, but he's still holding my gaze.

"No. But, he broke in! I was warned about this gentleman three days ago..."

The captain raises a hand and the cashier goes quiet. At the cusp of the dock, the ship hands have come to stand still, watching us—unsure if they're needed. The captain says, "Get going, Cook." And he nods out, toward the road.

I stand there a moment longer.

"You either start moving, or we're gonna have a problem. I don't want that. Neither do you. Get moving."

I turn away, walking up to the street with my head bowed. Behind me, the ship's hands have started directing the line of traffic onboard. The wind isn't all that cold or sharp this morning, but it's managed to chafe my eyes, getting them watery so the world's a little muddled and confused.

Even before my legs start running, my brain is running—trying to figure out how to tread across the bay and beat the ferry back to Rockland.

Very suddenly it dawns on me—where I need to be. I know what I'm going to do, and I'm running; pumping my arms, running as fast as I can.

I run until every other sound fades away beneath the raw gasp of my breath.

I run until the world passing by barely registers—I just run, thinking only of Ray.

36

The insides of my nose and throat are singed, but I'm still running when I come down the long stretch of the Rutter's driveway. Cramped up, but afraid to stop—afraid that if I stop I won't be able to get going again—I run past their truck and by the house.

Weak legged, I finally have to slow. But, the slowing feels like gravity—once it has me I know there's no getting free. I grab my side, groaning and hobbling, and by the time I get to the dock at the end of the property, I'm not running at all, just staggering along like an extra from *Night of the Living Dead*.

After tromping the length of the dock, I fall into the dingy tied alongside it. *The Bloody Rudder* is waiting, out in the current, only a few hundred feet from me and I can only hope, once I land there, that the Rutters have left the keys in it. If not, I think... My mind is blank from running. I gasp for air and tear the cover off the motor. The handle for the pull feels velveteen-plush under my fingers, but the resistance from the cord is like I'm trying to turn the world with it.

The flywheel whispers its round, but doesn't start. I prime the tank and pull again—and again there's a breezy flutter of noise, but no resulting life. I prime again and pull the choke. This time pulling the cord calls up a clamor, the engine shaking and coughing before working itself to a purr. I turn to the line lashed to the dock, the rope falling free willingly, once I loosen the first twist. My hand's just landing on the second rope, when a big blast of noise breaks the air, stopping me still.

Todd Rutter's out the front door, starting down the path from the house, lowering his shotgun barrel to meet me, shouting, "Cut that fucking engine!"

I lean back, killing the switch. The engine sputters out and in the resumed silence my breath and heart beat seem louder than the splash of waves. Todd's footsteps, coming down the gravely incline of the driveway are louder than the sucking of the sea.

"Tie that fucking line!" he yells.

I tie the line.

"Get out." He's not even yelling now, just commanding lazily, as though bored, as though he always knew our relationship would culminate in something like this. He's got a wicked bruise around his eye and it makes me smile, even as I'm shaking from the threat of the gun, trying to climb from the wobbly table of the boat on my weak legs. He shakes his head. We're both on the dock now, just at our first steps onto it and he's shaking his head as he paces out the distance between us. So close, he lets the gunstock fall to his waist. "You must have some fucking death wish, Cookie."

"Don't call me that."

"What's that?"

"Nothing. Never mind," I say.

"I oughta just fucking shoot you. I oughta put you outta your damn misery. Who'd fucking care?"

I shrug, looking away to the black water beside me.

"Would anyone fucking care?"

I think, Meredith and Drew, maybe—but it's hard imagining my memory being anything like lasting or cherished for either of them. I shake my head. "Probably not."

"What the fuck are you doing out here, you crazy asshole?"

"I need to get back to the mainland," I say, the old panic, the sense of necessity, of purpose, of time ticking down to a resolution I cannot accept, bubbling up anew.

"Take the fucking ferry, you fucking clod-brained mother-fucker. What the fuck are you doing trying to steal my boat?"

"I told you, I need to get back to the mainland. I need to beat the ferry back there," I say and, unsure that I've stressed the point adequately, I repeat, "I need to."

"Need to?" he says—it has the ring of a taunt. "Need to?"

I say, "You have a brother. You know what it's like having a brother; you know that, right? Well, I'm telling you, I gotta save my brother. He's in real danger, Todd. Bad danger."

He shakes his head. "Cookie, your brother's dead."

I nod. "To most people."

He looks at me, unblinking for a moment. "What are we gonna do about this?"

"Gimme a ride."

"Fuck off. Not that," he says, hitching the barrel of the gun in the direction of the dingy. "This. You trying to steal my boat."

"Gimme a ride."

"Get off that. It won't happen. I oughta shoot you, is what I oughta do," he says. His brother has come out of the house now, too, the storm door clapping behind him as he bounds down the weatherworn steps. "I ain't gonna. I oughta. But, I won't," he says and seems to think. "Call the cops, that's what I'll have to do."

"Don't, please," I say.

"We're well beyond 'please' getting anyone anywhere, Cookie."

"Please."

"You fucking jumped me twice. You trespassed here twice. You're trying to steal my fucking boat. What would you do?"

"Take me ashore."

"I told you: get off that. It's a fucking dream. It's not gonna happen."

"I'll give you anything."

"I wouldn't take it." He scoffs, "Besides, you haven't got anything." My hand is shaking when I pull the check out of my pocket, when I reach out to him with it. "What the fuck is that?"

"Take it."

He turns the gun aside and snaps the check from my hand. He shakes the check a moment to get it to lay straight in the wind. At first he looks stunned and then amused. "I see. It's a fucking joke. You got some balls making a fucking joke with a gun on ya."

"It's five thousand dollars," I say.

"Written to 'Cash?' No one writes a five thousand dollar check to 'Cash,' Cookie. You'd have to be retarded."

"Look at the name. Look at the last name."

He works to straighten the check out again, looks at it, shaking his head. Biting his lip.

Suddenly, breaking the conference between us, the younger brother is there, clomping down the dock, squeezing his fists vigorously, coming to step by his brother. Todd barres the way with the barrel of the shotgun. Not-Todd holds up abruptly, his gaze turning from the barrel at his waist to his brother's face. They share a look and Todd hands him the check.

Not-Todd just looks confused. "What the fuck is this?"

"Get-out-of-jail-free-card, I guess. Take it up to the house."

Not-Todd doesn't argue. He looks at me once, briefly, returning his attention to the check, where his eyes wander over it, again and again in the same pattern. With his head bowed like a sleepwalker, his eyes bound to the check, he turns back to the house. Todd lets the barrel of the gun fall and nods at the boat, "In."

Stepping down into the dingy, I go to the bow and take my seat. Todd gets in, crossing the gun over his lap. "I have a brother, too. I'm sorry for you that yours is gone." He holds my gaze. He says, "Seriously though, no more bullshit from you."

I nod.

"Don't have me regret this."

I shake my head.

He bends around to start the motor. The engine comes alive instantly for him and he nods for me to untie my line and when I have, he pushes off and twists the throttle and we cut a shallow arc out into the bay toward the *Bloody Rudder*.

37

By the time Rockland can be seen, the North Haven ferry is finally in sight, appearing to sit, stopped as we rush toward it. Growing larger and larger, we descend on her with Todd holding the throttle of *The Bloody Rudder* to its near limit.

I catch sight of the Prius and a glimpse of Priscilla's spiny hair as we cruise by. We're only slightly out in front when Todd eases back on the engine. Almost to port, I rush to the bow, ready to jump to the little marina dock that juts out next to the ferry terminal. I'm barely balanced when Todd brings us abruptly down to speed—the bow of the boat sinking suddenly, so that I have to flag my arms to keep from going into the drink. Todd chitters behind me. Eased near the dock, I jump off.

"Good luck, what ever crazy-ass-shit it is you're doing," Todd calls to me before backing the boat out and roaring off.

The ferry lands against the dock a long minute later. The deck hands start darting around, lashing up the ship.

With my toes at the cusp of the asphalt I stand and wait. There is nothing to do but wait while the chains at the bow are drawn aside and passengers start filing out.

The Prius is the first car off, humping and shrugging off the ramp into the lot. I stare back at Priscilla as she lays eyes me. I must have some grave look on my face, when I step up on the pavement, into her path—she's as pale as I've ever seen her. Turning to Tomothy, the two exchange some words.

I expect them to accelerate, to wind up and move to the outside lane and whip past me, but after she's looked forward again, the Prius slides out from the head of the queue, coming to stop a few yards beside me in the turnoff for the marina.

From under glass, unbuckling his seatbelt, Tomothy raises a hand in salute, going for the door handle as I come around to Priscilla's window. Seeing my reflection, I just don't blame her for thinking it over hard before she rolls the window half-down.

"Mr. Cook," she says. Her voice is shaky and her eyes move to my fists, which have curled closed.

"Witch, I want you to listen to me," I tell her. I'm trembling, trying to hold myself back. "I think I forgot, somewhere along the way, where it was I wanted to end up. So much time's passed now, I'm sure I can't start over again. I can't change what I've done. Or, who I am. But, I think I can still change how I act, so that to somebody, someday, maybe, I'll look like a better person than the person standing here. At least somewhat. I have to believe, at the very least, I can become someone, who, in a circumstance such this, wouldn't drag someone like you out of her car and slap her upsidedown until she gives me what the fuck I want. So, I'm willing to experiment here and see how pacifism might work for me."

She nods. Tomothy has come around to the hood of the car, to watch me from outside the range of my arms.

"I'm gonna ask you one goddamned time to open your trunk and I expect you to do it." I tell her, "Being peaceful is new to me and I don't honestly know how I'll react if it fails."

She says, "It still seems a little like a threat, when you word it like that." At the back of the car, I hear the hatchback pop. "Just a constructive criticism."

The steamer trunk's still there, crouching in shadows. I fumble with the latch and when it won't release, I wrestle the box up, out of the back of the car and let it fall to the ground. It lands with a muted whomp—like a sound coming up from deep water. Tomothy steps forward, saying, urgently, "Don't break it. It isn't locked."

I already have my foot cocked up, ready to unleash it on the box. I stand a moment, wobbling, before setting my boot back down. I step back. Tomothy has stopped still, staring at me. "Well?" I say. "Fucking open it."

The boy nods quickly, rushing forward, keeping an eye on me as he crouches down to snap loose the latch. The lid springs up an inch. Tomothy looks at me a moment, over the top of the box, before I hitch my head to the side and he scampers out of my way.

I take his place by the steamer trunk. Dropping to my knees, I toss the lid up. Inside is all blue-green, like the ocean in summer. Plunging my hands in, I grab at tufts of blue and pull, throwing handfuls aside. I grab and pull and throw, pull and throw, littering the air and the ground with long streamers of blue that come from the mouth of the trunk endlessly, while I call out, "Ray? Ray?"

Only there is an end. There is a bottom. And when my hands scrape it, I realize that what I'm pulling out is just cloth. Panting, I look at the ground around my knees littered with blouses and sweaters, blue jeans. I'm trembling. Turning back to the pair, I scream, "Where is he?!"

"He's gone," Tomothy says softly.

"What did you do with him?!"

"Your brother's gone, Barry. He's passed on," Priscilla tells me.

I've gotten off my knees and I'm crouched low now, all my weight resting on my ankles in a pose ready to launch, ready to attack. Maybe I'm trembling too much. My legs give out and I fall, hard on my ass, my back landing against the plastic bumper of the Prius.

They don't move. They watch me.

All I can do is ask, "Why?"

"Everything is temporary, Mr. Cook," Priscilla, says.

Tomothy nods and is quiet while Priscilla comes to me, bending down, laying a hand on my shoulder and squeezing and though I expect her to remove her hand, she does not. She lets it rest, a long pause before she squeezes again and I look up at her. Her face is smudgy and out-of-focus.

"You'll be okay, Barry." She squeezes again. "We all have to let go. Learning to let go is the greatest lesson of life. Life reminds us over and over how to let go; that we must let go."

I feel myself shrink under the unbearably light weight of her touch.

Ray is gone. Ray has been gone a very long time. I'm filled with grief. I shouldn't ever have left him on the island, alone. As though privy to my thoughts, Priscilla tells me, "There is nothing you could have done. He's just gone, Barry. He's just gone."

I push her hand away.

38

It must be very late or something; I am drunk.

Although, when I look at the clock, I'm disconcerted to find that it is not late at all—it is eight-thirty and I'm sitting, precariously at the bar of the Electric Company. There are a few patrons behind me, the sound of conversation weak enough so that, even with my eyes closed and all my concentration focused, I can't make out more than a word here, a phrase there. The conversation means nothing—not to me and not, so far as I can tell, to any context outside of me. It's all gibberish, untethered to meaning. The bartender has chosen a station at the other end of the bar, his elbow propped up and holding a copy of *The Trial*, that nonsense Kafka book.

When I raise a finger to indicate I'd like another drink he doesn't even move. I close my eyes and slump forward and wonder about Nevers.

Money. His money was bad money, I try to make myself feel better about the fact that it isn't mine any longer—that it was, only for the quickest blink of an eye. Just words written out on paper. A promise, a hope, that turned into nothing-much-at-all, air and dust. As hopes sometimes do.

"You want another?"

I open my eyes to find the bartender has reappeared before me. I tell him, "Two."

He pours me one, as though I hadn't spoken and returns to his book.

In three champion gulps I down the beer and wag my finger. The barman's become so versed, so practiced in ignoring me that when I fail to get his attention the first time, I don't bother trying again. On shifty legs, I go to the back of the bar where there's an ancient English pay-phone booth; the phone it was built to hold, predictably absent. Dragging myself inside, I fumble with the wood and glass bifold. It hiccups and catches. Looking up from his book the bartender frowns at me. At least, I think it's a frown. Through the muddling distance it's hard to tell.

I give him the finger and work the door all-the-way-shut.

My cell phone is almost dead, down to one blistery red bar of juice. But I do have service. I fumble through the buttons, making clumsy, wrong choices, backtracking to start again. Finally, I get it right. The ringing in my ear goes on almost too long. I'm ready to give up when Meredith says, "Hello."

"Hello," I say.

There's a pause. "Are you drunk, Barry?"

"As fuck."

There is another pause. "Are you okay?"

"I think I am," I say and I look at the clock and it's somehow gotten late. The bar is not full, but less empty than I remember it being. The clock on the wall says ten-thirty. "My brother's dead."

"I know, Barry. I know."

"I think I'll sell the house."

"That's a good idea," she says. "You should probably stop drinking."

I nod.

"You still there?"

I nod.

"You should call your father. He's worried."

I nod.

"You still there?" I nod. She says, "Should I come get you before you get in a fight or something?"

"Probably."

"Where are you—Electric Company?"

"Probably."

"Is that a yes, Barry?"

There's a cold, constant wind that's blowing up Union Street, when I come out to wait for Meredith. When it blows sidelong against my ear, I think for a moment I can hear Ray's voice, rising up in it. It's his voice, I'm certain, but there aren't any words he's speaking, not any longer. There's just the resonance of him. I want to ask the wind about Sharon Wickworth. I want the wind to tell me about Suzy Trask's nipples and about bras hung from shotgun barrels. But, afraid of the silence that might follow, I try to be content, just listening to the sound of him.

~

It's a bright, blinding day when Meredith drives me toward the Knox County Jail, my future home for the next twelve to eighteen months. There's snow all over everything now. We're both quiet. I'm quiet because there's a big weight sitting on me. Meredith's quiet, I don't know, I suppose, because her last attempts at conversation have gone to stale silence. There's just nothing-much to say. I'm going to jail. I'm full of dread. The thump-thump of my lonely heart.

But, the house sold. And I guess that's good—I have a nest egg now, waiting for me when I get out. Pa was happy to hear about the sale, which I didn't expect, even though he was the one who gave me the keys and told me I should get rid of it.

I find, as we drive, listening to the road, that I'm mad at the day; pissed at the sunshine and the traffic around us, pissed at the people behind those windows and behind those wheels, who're heading someplace better than where I'm headed.

When I start feeling mad at Meredith over her silence, I have to remind myself that it's my doing. That all of this is my doing. All of it belongs to me and it's no one's burden but my own.

"You gonna come visit?"

"How many times you gonna ask me that?"

"Just tell me you're gonna come visit," I say.

"Yes, Barry," she says. "I'm gonna come visit. I bet you see a lot of Drew."

When I see the old, dull blue Coupe DeVille up ahead, pulled over onto the shoulder, I get Meredith to pull up behind it. "You gonna be sick?" she asks and I'm already getting out, not answering her. The Coupe DeVille's empty, but footsteps in the mushy snow lead out into the brush and beside the tracks is a drag mark. I step off the roadside, pushing branches away and following the tracks.

It's just a little ways in where I find the old man and his dog in a narrow clearing. The man has a patch of snow cleared away and he's trying to wedge the blade of a rusty shovel into the ground. The dog's laying on his side, at the end of the drag-rut in the snow. Grunting and sweaty, the old man's down to a t-shirt as he tries working the shovel. Only when Meredith comes to join us in the little clearing and says, "Oh, no," covering her mouth, does the old man look up.

"Barry Cook," he says and I nod. "Name's Everett..."

"You were a friend of my father's..."

"More of an acquaintance, really. Truth be told, I don't think he ever cared for me all that much," he says and leans against the shovel before turning down and going back to trying to stab the ground.

"I'm sorry to see your dog's gone."

"He was a good dog," he says between breaths. He's panting. His sweat steams in the cold day, a thin aura of fog enveloping him. "And we gotta bury our loved ones."

"I suppose that's right," I say and I'm already taking the shovel from him as I'm asking, "Mind if I have a turn? You look like you could use a break."

He lets go, trying to get his breath back, staggering off to stand by Meredith. He mops himself off with a sweater he's hung on a branch, before wrestling back into it.

"Barry," Meredith insists. "We don't want to be late."

I don't say anything, just start digging. The first six inches of ground is rock hard, but after that it gets easier—we're dead center in winter now, but a few intermittent thaws have kept the lower soil soft. I dig until I've got a notch in the ground big enough to hold the dog and I say, "You got anything you wanna say, before he goes in?"

"Got to finish the hole, first," the old man tells me.

I look at the hole. "Plenty wide."

"Wide isn't everything," he tells me. "Gotta be deep so he doesn't get dug up by reh'coons. If you're gonna do something you oughta have the decency to do it right."

I look at the hole. Getting back to digging, the shovel handle barely reaches out from within before Emmett will let me stop and call the job done. Meredith and I lower the mutt in and stand around while the old man tells his dog that he was a good boy: loyal and un-finicky, both good traits, he points out, for a dog, or any animal. I push the soil back into the hole and when it's done and the ground's got a big brown blister on it, I straighten up and turn to find only Meredith standing there.

"Where'd he go?"

She shrugs. His car's gone, when we get back out onto the road.

The day has gotten thin, the brightness worn away, by the time she hugs me goodbye and I turn to the entrance of the jail to check myself in.

It is the same. Again and again. Everyday. We get a movie once a week, in black and white. Not the memorable ones, not historic films. The plots of these make little sense: formal people in formal attire using strange, senseless slang. Always a narrator frantically speaking to bridge the lack of cohesion. I just stare at the flickering images, without sensing that any of it means much-of-anything-at-all.

Pa comes to visit after I've been in for a month. He looks different. Tanned and without his beard, it takes his wide smile before I recognize him. After talking awhile, near the end of his visit, he invites me to live with him in Florida, when I'm out. "The business is doing real well," he tells me. "Honestly, I could use a hand. It wouldn't be giving you a handout. Don't think that. I need the help. And I'll tell you, it's good work. Taking guys out fishing in the warm. Not like running the taxi. Nothing like that."

Drew comes and visits. Meredith, too. Sometimes they come together and sometimes separately, but every visiting day (once a week, that is) at least one of them is waiting for me. I find I do not like seeing them, that it makes the week in between seem longer and the hours just afterward painfully lonely. But, I don't tell them and they keep coming. At least part of me is happy that they do.

I'm inside some few months before I'm approached in the cafeteria by a man, laying his hand roughly on my shoulder. "She came back," he says. "She never went away." I shake the hand off and turn to find Nevers standing there. He looks worse than before. He's missing one of his front teeth now, the mirror same of the one I don't have.

"Get away from me," I tell him. It feels like a bad dream, his being here.

I avoid him at every occasion and eventually he stops hounding me and turns into just another face. Eventually it seems like he's forgotten who I am, altogether. We have no bond anymore. Nothing between us. We're strangers.